Channel Tides

CJ Smith was born in Reading and studied Microbiology at Newcastle and Theology at Oxford. Before ordination, he worked promoting the Alpha Course at Holy Trinity, Brompton. He served as a curate in Cambridge, then as an associate minister in Manchester, Vermont, USA. For ten years he was Rector of Chevening in Kent, and he now serves as Rector of Marlborough. Having worked for churches for more than three decades, he remains committed to helping people and congregations grow in their knowledge and love of Jesus.

Married to Catherine, with whom he has four children, CJ loves walking his dog, travelling, and talking with anyone who will listen about life and faith. He writes with a prophetic edge, encouraging others to think deeply, live generously, and find joy in the story that God is writing. *Channel Tides* is his first novel.

Channel Tides

When Hope Takes The Helm

CJ Smith

Blackbird Press

First published in Great Britain November 2025

Blackbird Press
The Rectory
Marlborough
Wiltshire SN8 1AU
blackbirdpress25@gmail.com

ISBN 978-1-9193534-2-5

Dedicated to
Adam Smith and Graham Turner

Chapter 1
The First Crossing

The rising sun over Deal was a sight that never grew old to the Vicar. His black Labrador, Tess, loved it too; she'd have been in the water all day if he'd let her.

One April morning was particularly chilly and clear. The sun was close to rising, but for now the horizon blurred; land and sea almost indistinguishable in the dawn light. Tess began barking, far too early for the neighbours. The Vicar hurried over, shushing as he went, but when she suddenly fell silent, he froze.

There was no mistaking it. A body. It looked like a woman, face down, dark-skinned, half on the beach and half in the sea.

The Vicar bent down, gripped her shoulders and pulled with all his strength until she lay fully on the shingle. Even in death she looked young and beautiful.

He sank to his knees beside her, gave Tess a treat and then pulled out his phone. He rang '999' as the coastguard needed to know. He was almost certain she was a migrant who must have attempted a dinghy crossing that had gone horribly wrong. The tides of the English Channel had brought her to Deal. But why? The questions kept rising in his chest: Who was she? Where had she come from? What had her home been like? What was her name?

Quietly, he began to pray the Lord's Prayer, then laid his hand gently on her cold body and spoke the words of *The Committal*. When he finished, he lifted his eyes to the breaking dawn and said aloud,

'Lord, please stop this madness.'

Chapter 2
The Buccaneers' Bar

…Two years later

At the top of the golf club stairs, the Buccaneers' Bar looked out over the Channel, three sides of glass framing the restless water. In the centre stood a square bar, ceiling and floor mirroring one another so that no matter where you sat, you could see through to the sea. Naval ships and pirate prints hung on the walls, with Frederick Waugh's *The Buccaneers* in pride of place.

This was where Alan came most evenings, to meet the three men his wife Leslie called the 'panel of experts'. Alan liked to think of them as simply gentlemen of experience. There was Bill, moustached, ex-Navy, his career still wrapped in secrecy; Dave, a Geordie who had once marketed Furbies and never stopped with the one-liners; and Colin, an engineer with a taste for gadgets. Golf was an occasional excuse. Meeting up at The Buccaneers' Bar was the friends' priority.

They put the world to rights over pints, often with more confidence than accuracy. Alan, the organiser of the group, had already launched 'Pothole Watch Kent'. Lately the state of the roads seemed less of a problem than the boats. A week earlier, Alan and Leslie, out in their cruiser *The Lady Kathleen*, had been jostled by a dinghy full of migrants. 'Forty-six of them!' he told the others. 'They asked for fuel. I told them to sod off and get it in France. Leslie, the softie, gave them a jerry can. So that's another forty-six on our shores – thanks to me!'

The others chuckled, but Bill's face tightened. He had seen too much at sea to laugh easily. Colin nodded along; Dave quipped something about invasions. Beneath the humour was unease.

Wives and girlfriends were tolerated at The Buccaneers' on special occasions. Colin's Miranda talked endlessly about their children; Dave's Laura dragged herself in from her exhausting days at a Margate primary school; Bill's companions came and went, what with his restless life at sea. Only Leslie seemed at ease. She liked that Alan had his outlet and Alan liked that she had hers: St George's Church.

He didn't go himself. There had been a rupture years ago, one of those private matters men don't discuss in a bar, and he'd never quite gone back. But on Sunday nights he liked hearing Leslie's summary of the sermon over a drink on their terrace. It was the one thing he missed about church: the chat afterwards over coffee.

He had noticed that the new vicar, unlike the previous 'sandal-wearing beardo', preached a lot less about the climate and politics and more about the state of people's souls and their character. Alan found that quite refreshing and was not entirely surprised when Leslie repeated this Sunday's challenge:

'Don't think about the good you cannot do, but rather the good you can do.'

Alan scoffed at first, but its pithiness stuck with him. That night he found it hard to sleep. By Monday evening, when he sank onto his bar stool, he was restless.

'What's got your goat?' Colin asked.

'Leslie and her church again. The vicar's been on at them saying they should do the good they can, not moan about the good they can't.'

They smiled. ‘What would we talk about then?’ said Dave. But as the humour faded, Bill looked up from his pint; ‘I could stop those small boats,’ he said confidently. ‘France won’t. Our government can’t. But if it were down to us…I know I could.’

The words hung in the air. Alan looked at Bill, noticing the tautness in his shoulders, the calm certainty in his eyes. This wasn’t idle bravado. This was a man who meant it. Slowly, the others let the moment settle. Colin sipped his beer, Dave tilted back in thought, Alan’s mind already turning over the possibilities.

For the first time, the idea of doing something began to emerge as more than just banter. The suggestion had promise and purpose. And somehow, in the quiet hum of the bar and the restless view of the Channel beyond, it felt like the beginning of something that could matter.

Chapter 3
The Pashtun Pharmacist

Abdul was tall enough to see over most customers' heads, dark enough to be mistaken for someone older than he felt. Much to his private frustration he was incapable of growing a proper beard. Not that he cared about vanity. It was just one of life's little injustices, like electricity cutting out at the worst moment, or shelves that never stayed straight no matter how carefully you tidied them.

He helped run his father's pharmacy in Lashkargah, the capital of the Afghan region of Helmand. It was right by the Chawk Cinema, which meant the street was always alive: the smell of fried bread curling from the corner shop, children weaving through traffic with shoes too big for their feet, scooters zipping past, horns blaring. The pharmacy itself was modest but perfectly placed: a small glass frontage, shelves crammed with imported and local medicines, a humming fridge that worked when it wanted to. People came in to buy, to ask advice, or just to talk; Abdul treated them all the same.

He loved his community. He knew their ailments, their stubbornness, their small dramas. A mother fretted over a cough. A man haggled over paracetamol. Abdul listened warmly and gave what he could; sometimes free, sometimes for the little cash they had. Competent, careful, respectful; a professional in a town that could be chaotic.

But the world was changing. Since the Taliban had returned, life had grown harder. Savings dwindled. Stock grew scarce. Banks couldn't lend. Every day, Abdul ran the numbers in his head: rent, electricity, suppliers, medicines. Like juggling knives: drop one and it cut deep.

And then there was the family. His father was ageing and increasingly reliant on him to keep the shop open; to keep life in order. His brother had long gone to the UK, sending occasional photos and messages. Abdul loved them both. His family was his anchor. If he stayed, he could preserve the pharmacy and care for his father. If he left maybe he could secure their future, assuming he survived the journey.

'Zaranj' was whispered on the edges of conversation. The first step toward Europe: dusty roads, smugglers, bribes, danger that kept most people indoors. Abdul hadn't decided yet; the idea lingered, shadowy at the back of his mind. He pictured the journey, the people, the risks. And the chance to rebuild something better: a pharmacy that could thrive.

Could he leave? Could he trust the world beyond Lashkargah, beyond the friends he knew, beyond streets he could navigate blindfolded? Could he survive the smugglers, the borders, the uncertainties? He didn't know. All he knew was that the pharmacy needed capital, his father needed him, and in the small hours, when the electricity failed and the fridge stopped, he wondered what a man should do when all roads seemed necessary and dangerous.

Abdul straightened a shelf, nudged a row of bottles back into place and exhaled. Tonight, the question of leaving could wait. Tonight, he would serve those who came through his door, listen to their concerns, laugh with them at the absurdities of life. And sometimes, that was enough. Hope lingered in the air, like the smell of bread drifting down the street: proof, if only small, that the world was not yet lost.

Chapter 4
The Cornfield Campus

Naylor University rose politely out of the Indiana fields, as though corn and soybeans had simply stepped aside to make room. A cluster of red-brick buildings with white trim stood amid manicured lawns, banners fluttering with 'Faith, Service, Excellence.' It was the kind of place where litter never lingered and even the bicycles seemed polished. Students were healthy, radiantly so and the air buzzed with ambition and good cheer.

Naylor was a Christian liberal arts college, proud of its heritage and thriving under its new president, David Wincey. Four years of study was the usual rhythm, but students were expected to break that rhythm with service: a mission trip in the summer after their second year and perhaps a semester abroad in their third year through the Lighthouse Programme. The brochures glittered with options: Uganda, Peru, Thailand, inner-city Chicago – glossy promises of adventure and transformation.

But one option didn't quite fit. Three months in England, attached to St George's Church in Deal. Schools, Sunday services with tea and biscuits, parish life by the sea. It was hardly the Serengeti or the Amazon. The placement existed, it seemed, because the vicar of St George's was an old friend of Naylor's president. Opportunities sometimes came less by grand design than by friendship.

Among those scanning the Lighthouse list were two unlikely candidates for England.

Micah Wildman came from Fort Stockton, Texas. Short, blonde, compact and strong. He was the kind of young man who always looked as if he were about to spring into action. But there was more to him than muscle. He had wanted to join the Marines, like his two older brothers, but his eyesight, the kind that couldn't quite be fixed, had closed that door. He told people he had accepted it, trusting that the Lord knew best. But the ache to serve never really left him. His mother, a retired actress, worried for him. His father had served in the military as well; they didn't want him to feel what he'd choose would be second best. At Naylor, what stood out wasn't just his Southern manners – the constant 'Sir' and 'Ma'am' that softened his voice – but his readiness to help. If he was a dog, he'd be a Golden Retriever. He tinkered with friends' broken phones, resuscitated gadgets and never made anyone feel foolish for asking.

Micah studied physics and engineering, relishing the puzzle of how things worked. Yet what really marked him out was his loyalty. His friends knew he'd turn up when it mattered, toolbox in hand or simply with an encouraging word. He thought his family might have had roots in Kent and the idea of returning there, however indirectly, stirred something in him; part heritage, part unfinished longing.

Gabriella Martinez came from Bloomfield Hills, Michigan. Her mother was Canadian, her father ran a construction firm, and she was the middle of five children: two older sisters, already setting the pace and two younger brothers scrambling to keep up. She was Midwestern through and through; calm and clear, with an instinctive politeness and a smile that put people at their ease.

People noticed Gabriella not only for her looks but also for her poise. She listened well, thought before speaking and in a college full of confident voices, that gave her a kind of gravity. One of her sisters was a television weather presenter, but Gabriella's gift was steadiness. She studied psychology and was leaning towards children's welfare. She had patience for the young and curiosity for their stories. She loved words, her own and others. At Naylor that made her valuable in a hundred different ways.

Both Micah and Gabriella belonged to prayer triplets, which Naylor encouraged. The idea was to be honest with this small group about the highs and lows of life and bring all of it to God in prayer. Both asked their triplets for help as to where they should spend their Lighthouse time. Uganda and Peru sounded obvious, Thailand exotic, Chicago gritty. England sounded odd – almost comic. But the idea wouldn't quite leave them alone. For Micah, England was ancestral ground. For Gabriella, it was the land of *Miss Marple* reruns and voices she secretly imitated. Deal lacked glamour, but it carried a tug neither could ignore.

They prayed and talked to friends. Gabriella thought English schools might show her something new about childhood. Micah wondered, half-seriously, whether the adventure the Marines had denied him might be waiting for him in Kent.

So, when the time came to click their choices, both put St George's, Deal, England at the top of their list. The screen gave no hint of acceptance. But afterwards, both felt the faint, nervous thrill of having chosen the less obvious road.

Chapter 5
The Buccaneers' Vision

Alan leaned back on his bar stool, absently swirling the amber liquid in his glass. 'We should all have a think about this and come back to it on Wednesday,' he said, half in jest, half as a nudge.

Bill didn't need the nudge. He had been turning the idea over in his head for weeks, since he'd been retired by the Navy. Countermeasures, patrol patterns, timings – he could almost see it all in his mind's eye. The only missing pieces were funding and the civilian workforce, neither of which was his strong suit. Experience had taught him one thing: if you needed something, you asked the brass for exactly what was required, then left them to work out what they could deliver. He'd do the same here, in a new setting

Dave, as usual, was unsure where he fitted in. He wanted to help, of course, but mostly felt like a spectator at the edge of something larger. A slight pang of inadequacy nagged him; he could offer enthusiasm and a quick quip, but how much did that count?

Alan's tidy mind was already whirring with spreadsheets, rosters and the faint thrill of operational possibility. Colin's tinkerer brain was alive with drones, surveillance equipment and gadgets he could modify to suit the plan. Together, their business acumen and engineering flair complemented Bill's operational know-how, but they were reliant on him to chart the course.

By Wednesday evening, anticipation had morphed into quiet tension. The bar hummed with the usual background chatter, but at the square in the middle, the four men were focused. Bill cleared his throat. 'Right,' he said, voice low but steady, 'Here's how this could work.'

First, he headlined the mission: 'Our aim is to stop all small-boat crossings of the English Channel.' Old habits die hard and he repeated this as if he was back addressing his troops. Then he added the reasoning to give it moral force: 'It's unsafe, it's breaking the law and it's making the Navy look ridiculous.' He was preaching to the choir but he left a space to see if anyone wanted to underline or object. Dave jumped in, 'What's all the carry on at Gatwick for, all that Passport Control, if we just let these people in willy nilly?' Alan and Colin exchanged a look and Bill assured them: 'We'll get to money and legals in a minute.'

Bill moved on to strategy: 'I've been on a recce and the way forward is simple: if you try to stop these dinghies mid-Channel, even more people will die. Their boats are rubbish; their life jackets are worse and lots of them can't swim. Once they've made it over to us, we can't get rid of them – they know that, which is why they keep coming. No, if you think it through, the obvious place to act is on the French beaches or in the shallows nearby as they load up. That's the safe place to stop them and if we can get a vice-grip on that for a few months, eventually they'll stop coming.'

When he said 'vice-grip' a small shiver of recognition ran through the group; Bill's tone carried the authority of experience. The obvious next questions – the how, the legalities, the costs – would wait until the next round.

Even with their differing financial situations, they were religious about sharing the cost of beer. Two rounds, as ever, before heading home for dinner. Colin caught the barmaid's eye and ordered; Bill prepared to lay out the finer details.

Chapter 6
Journeys Begin

Abdul lingered in the pharmacy that had been his father's life. The walls smelled faintly of antiseptic and old wood; the counters lined with glass jars and labelled boxes he had memorised as a child. His father moved slowly, counting pills, checking stock, trying to keep the shop running despite the dwindling savings and impossibility of borrowing money under Taliban rule.

Abdul had watched his elder brother leave for the UK in search of opportunity, but for him this was different. He didn't want to vanish like that. He wanted to make an active choice and he wanted it to be a family moment.

That evening, they gathered at the small courtyard behind the pharmacy. The family prepared food with care: bread baked over coals, spiced lamb and tea poured into small glass cups. Abdul's father said little, his pride and worry threaded through each measured movement. Abdul's heart ached at the sight of him, yet he knew he could not stay. The shop would need him eventually, but if he delayed, the opportunity and the chance to help his family, might slip away entirely.

They ate together, their voices low, laughter mixing with tears. Abdul felt the weight of his decision settle around him, heavy, yet strangely comforting. By the end of the evening, there was a sense of solidarity, a silent promise that this departure was not abandonment, but a step toward securing their future.

Early the next morning, Abdul packed his small bag, kissed his parents and set out for Zaranj. The cool streets were just waking, vendors calling softly and the border in the distance, which promised the first leg of a long and uncertain journey.

As he walked, he rehearsed the plans he had already begun to make in his mind: the route, the smugglers, the contacts. But more than that, he carried the warmth of the farewell meal, a memory that would sustain him through what lay ahead.

***

Meanwhile, halfway across the globe in Indiana, another journey of purpose was quietly beginning. Students at Naylor University were packing for home, but for 120 third-year students waiting by their phones, the morning held one more pulse-quickening ritual: the Lighthouse Programme allocation. From the mission centre, emails were dispatched at exactly the same moment, timed to coincide with morning chapel. Pings erupted across dorms and libraries, a cascade of digital confetti. Students glanced at each other, eyes wide, fingers hovering over screens.

Micah's phone pinged first. He clicked, heart thudding and scanned the message. Amongst the generalities of the email was the key information: Kent, England. Summer term at St George's, Deal. A smile tugged at the corner of his mouth.

Gabriella's screen lit up simultaneously: Kent. She blinked, reading and rereading the words. Her chest tightened in a flutter of excitement, along with the faint, nagging awareness that this meant fundraising, planning and stepping into the unknown.

They sat next to each other in chapel, glancing occasionally at their phones tucked discreetly in their laps. The chaplain spoke about prayer and purpose. Each student was encouraged to pray for their Lighthouse placement, for the people they would meet, the work they would do and the journey of faith ahead. Most students were headed off much sooner in January; the summer term felt like a distant horizon at that moment.

Micah and Gabriella exchanged quick smiles, sensing that whatever awaited them in Kent was bigger than a summer programme, though neither could yet say exactly what. The morning sunlight glinted through the chapel windows, hinting at possibilities.

Chapter 7
Flesh on the Ribs

As they began their second pints, Bill pressed on with the details. He spoke in short, efficient sentences, the cadence of someone used to briefing men who had to act on what they heard. He had brought four sheets of A5 with a reminder of the headlines.

'Patrollers,' he began. 'Pleasure craft. Motor cruisers that can comfortably make the trip to Calais and back. All running from Ramsgate. A crew of five, including the owners. They sail fast in the first hour to the French coast, then very slowly the last few miles into Calais – they hover. After someone's bought a pastry, a bottle of wine they head slowly back out, keeping the receipt of course. Once they're right offshore, then full speed for home. On the slow bits near Calais, recon drones are flown from them to spot smuggler activity. Three boats per watch covering Northern, Central and Southern sectors. One early shift, leaving at four in the morning, back at three in the afternoon. A later shift, leaving at two, back at ten pm. They don't go at night and they don't go if the waves are bigger than ¾ of a metre.'

Colin was already drawing a little map. 'The trips are plausibly holiday outings,' he said. 'And you could be filming the coast for your Instagram. People won't bat an eyelid, what could they stop you for?' Dave, who was reading ahead, asked: 'And the Scouts?'

‘Campers,’ Bill said. ‘Early retirees with campervans. They park up in Northern France “birdwatching” and touring, but really they’ll be keeping an eye on the beaches and launching hotspots. No fancy kit needed; just binoculars and a phone that works in France. I’m assuming they can drop a pin on WhatsApp. They’ll travel in pairs for morale. If they see smuggler activity, say on the canals, they ping the Patrollers. While one of the crew carries on the recon, two others launch “puncture drones”, which do what they say on the tin.’ Bill noticed a look of surprise, ‘Yes, it's military spec kit but they only puncture boats not people – don’t worry!’

‘And the Ribs?’ Alan asked, the word hanging oddly in the air.

Bill slowed but did not soften. ‘Rigid Inflatable Boats. Fast and manoeuvrable. Military drivers. Crews of two or three. They station themselves just inside our territorial waters. They linger there until the signal comes from the Scouts and the Patrollers. Then, and this will be my role, we make like hell for the coast before the dinghies are launched. Once we get there, we have a few extra methods at our disposal to disable the dinghies before they clear shallow water. The key thing is to stop the migrants from setting off. And if no one sets off…’

‘No one arrives,’ Alan added.

‘And no one drowns,’ said Dave.

‘Exactly!’ said Bill.

Colin’s pen paused. ‘How many patrol boats?’

‘Ideally a pool of twenty-four,’ Bill said. ‘Three on Monday morning, three Monday afternoon. Repeat on Thursday. Different crews on Tuesday and Friday; different again on Wednesday and Saturday. Sundays managed separately. And we’ll want three reserves just in case.’

‘How many Scouts?’ Dave asked. He wanted numbers because for him they made things less alarming.

‘Four Scouts per week,’ Bill said. ‘Ideally two couples go over in two vans. Pair One take a three-day trip and Pair Two take a four-day trip. If each van goes once per month we need sixteen campers in total. Camping any more than once a month would start to look suspicious.’

‘And the Ribs?’ Colin asked.

‘Three plus a support vessel. Patroller Captains and Scouts can all be civvies; we want them to be as unnoticed as possible. But the drone crews, the Rib crews and the support team all need to be ex-military. They can’t be volunteers fresh from the golf club. Add HQ staff in Ramsgate and it’s about 22 hired personnel per shift.’

Alan had started to organise in his head. ‘Where do the drones come from?’

Colin smiled a little, the tinkerer’s grin. ‘I don’t only make parts for solar panels at the factory.’ He tapped his napkin. He could make them. He could modify them. He had plenty of ideas.

‘And the Ribs?’ Alan asked, the accountant in him bracing for the line he knew would hurt.

‘Half a million each,’ Bill said without flinch. ‘Three needed to start. We can rent the support vessel. Total equipment cost: say two million. Weekly running costs – staff, fuel, vessels, maintenance, accommodation – all in about 90k.’

Bill knew that this was the worst case; it could be less. But he’d learnt with the brass over the years: quote worse than reality, as they hate surprises.

Dave’s face went slack. ‘That’s… a lot of money.’

Bill nodded. It was the part he expected people to baulk at. ‘The network exists. I have contacts to get crew. But people have to be paid. If we’re going to succeed, we need a proper budget, proper people and a proper plan.’

Colin put down his pen. ‘Is this legal?’ His voice had a thin edge.

Bill shrugged one heavy shoulder. 'Depends on where you are. In UK waters, we'll flirt with legalities but probably be fine if we keep it civilian. Once in French waters, I don't know. I've structured it so the civilians can plausibly deny any involvement. For paid help, that's a different problem. We'll have to ask Legal Lee.'

At the name, the others groaned in unison. Legal Lee, rotund, eloquent, a club member with a taste for hearing his own voice. He was a successful local lawyer they all tried to avoid on the golf course. Alan gave a rueful look of surrender. 'I'll take one for the team. I'll book him in.'

They circled back to money. Colin and Alan looked at each other. Both were self-made and had done well, but this was not small change. Colin jumped in this time, 'Why don't Alan and I have a chat after that round with Legal Lee?'

'And the wives?' Dave said hesitantly. 'How and when do we tell them?'

Alan's mouth tightened. He had already imagined these conversations: spreadsheets next to family dinners, explanations on terraces, worried faces. The moral case would be strong, but legal and marital consent really mattered. 'We'll talk to Legal Lee. We'll get proper numbers. Then we discuss it with wives and girlfriends.'

'Best not to start a domestic before we know what we're getting into,' Dave joked.

As it was England, the weather came up. Bill had notes ready: crossings are likelier in calm water. More pleasant in summer but attempted all year, so long as the swell is under ¾ metre. There would be down days and cancellations, times when nothing happened. For volunteers, boredom could be as frequent as adrenaline.

'And what if people get hurt?' Dave asked before he could stop himself.

‘It’s possible,’ Bill said plainly. ‘Lower risk for a trained team, but accidents happen. The smugglers aren’t running charities. They’re the ones really putting the migrants at risk. Last year, seventy-three died – and that’s just the bodies they found. But if we accept stopping the boats saves lives, we must also accept some risk. This operation could hurt people, even if we train and prepare for every eventuality.’

Bill’s bluntness left a taste. For a moment, the bar was quieter than it had been in years. The Channel glowered beyond the glass.

‘How long does it need to go on for?’ Alan asked finally. He had a spreadsheet in his head, a campaign calendar.

‘Nine months,’ Bill said. ‘If we can make the crossings unviable for the whole spring and summer, then the business model collapses. And if the smugglers go, the migrants won’t come. That’s the aim.’

They ran through a rough scale of commitment. On a scale from one to ten, Bill was ten. Alan and Colin both said seven but could be pushed to ten if legal and financial questions were managed and their wives agreed. Dave said eight but still had not found his precise place; his peripheral eagerness both amused and warmed the others. Bill knew not to push further. It was a big commitment and people needed time to think it through.

They concluded with their brief plan: talk to Legal Lee, firm up finances, and then, with care, begin to talk to their other halves. Prudence masquerading as process. It felt oddly like the beginning of something that might, if all went well, matter in ways they hadn’t yet allowed themselves to imagine. The Channel went on as always, indifferent and patient. But in the square bar of Deal golf club four men had drawn a line in the sand and, for the first time, meant to walk towards it.

On Sunday night, Alan heard about the morning's sermon: 'Daring to be a Daniel,' Apparently, it was a talk for children encouraging them not to be afraid of walking into the Lion's den. Leslie liked the talks for children; they tended to have less padding. Alan felt it now, a mixture of dread and a strange exhilaration.

Chapter 8
Departures and Borders

Dorm rooms emptied, the crisp air smelled of leaves and pumpkin spice, and families arrived. Gabriella's father drove down in his truck to pick her up, the familiar rumble of the engine and smell of leather bringing a sense of home, even as she packed the last of her bags into the truck. Micah flew out from Indianapolis, first to Dallas, then connecting to Lubbock, where his older brothers, Jake and Matt, were waiting. They drove together back to Fort Stockton, teasing and arguing in the way only brothers can. As always, 'banter' was covering a multitude of sins.

The Naylor families always enjoyed Thanksgiving. It was like Christmas but with less stress. On Black Friday, some went shopping to see the latest 'doorbusters' that stores were offering to lure people over their thresholds. Meanwhile, Micah and Gabriella had their first virtual meeting with the Vicar in Deal. On the Zoom call, he showed them the accommodation at the Vicarage: each room had views of the church and Gabriella had her own bathroom. He smiled and invited them to pray together for the placement. Micah and Gabriella shared a brief moment of reflection, their minds already wandering to the classrooms they would enter and the children they would meet.

The Vicar wanted to reassure them that there was no fee for this mission trip; indeed, the church council had voted through a small stipend to cover their day-to-day expenses.

The practical details were comforting, but the weight of responsibility – speaking of faith to children aged five to eleven – was already beginning to take shape in their minds. They began to pray and think about how to communicate in ways that were clear, kind and fun.

Flight dates were fixed: April 11th to August 11th – easy to remember, at least. The Vicar and his wife shared that they'd lived in the States for four years, which made the connection feel warmer, more personal. Gabriella's father booked flights for her and her mother, turning the first week into a family adventure.

Meanwhile, Micah spent a few last hours with his grandfather, poring over old family documents. 'I think we came over from a village called Chilham,' his grandfather said, reading from yellowed papers. Kent, Micah realised, a place thousands of miles away, was already beginning to feel like a second home.

After the Thanksgiving break, it was back to classes; back to the rhythm of campus life, but the anticipation never left. They scheduled another chat with the Vicar in the New Year, giving them more time to plan and pray. The emails, the Zooms and the flights were all needed and yet both of them knew the real adventure hadn't even begun.

***

Far from Indiana, in a dusty Afghan border town, another departure was underway. Abdul arrived in Zaranj on one of the battered Afghan buses that trundled along the paved road the coalition had left behind. The seats were narrow, the suspension brutal, the air thick with exhaust fumes. But he hardly noticed, his mind was occupied with what lay ahead. Zaranj was a crossing point and from here the journey into Iran would begin.

The bus rattled to a stop at the terminal. Passengers disembarked, shouting and haggling over taxis and handcarts. Abdul stepped down and looked around, taking in the sun-bleached buildings and the crowds moving with purpose, each person carrying a story of their own. He felt a pang of homesickness, thinking of his father, the pharmacy, the city streets of Lashkargah, but reminded himself this was a choice he had made. Not to escape, but to prepare for a future where he might return and rebuild.

Through his brother's connections, he met the smugglers in a small, discreet café. The arrangements were swift and businesslike. Payment of $1,500 confirmed his passage across the border and all the way to Turkey. Every detail was laid out: the route through Iran, the timings, the contacts at each checkpoint. Abdul listened carefully, asking the questions that might ensure his safety.

When it was time to leave, he was ushered into a truck with a false floor, which was uncomfortable, if functional. The smugglers reassured him this was only for the border crossing, nothing more.

Before boarding, Abdul allowed himself one last glance at Zaranj. The town shimmered in the evening sun, ordinary and stubborn, like home itself. He did not know when he would see it again. The city, his family, his life – they were all behind him, and yet he carried them with him in his heart.

Chapter 9
The First Tee

Alan had never enjoyed golf with Legal Lee. The man was insufferable, bloated with his own cleverness and prone to treat every hole as a stage for his opinions. Still, Alan knew he needed him. So, when they shook hands on the first tee, Alan asked for confidentiality.

‘Oh, it’s like that, is it?’ Lee chuckled, winding Alan up. But when he caught his partner’s look, he straightened up. ‘Of course, of course.’

Alan explained the plan in simple, crisp sentences. That was his gift: to strip a problem down, slice off the fat and leave only what mattered. By the time his ball dropped neatly into the first hole, the shape of the operation was clear enough for Lee to grasp.

The lawyer was silent for a moment, then said: ‘Well. First off – brilliant. Brave. Someone has got to do something. It’s madness.’

It took eight holes for him to cover the legalities, his words spilling out faster than Alan could line up his shots. Maritime law, international law, the strange twilight status of the people crammed into those inflatable boats. ‘Likely stateless,’ Lee muttered at one point, ‘a fascinating conundrum!’ And on he went, delighted with his own insight. Alan let him ramble, knowing the man always needed a few fairways to circle the issue before he landed anywhere near a conclusion.

By the 11th hole Alan was pressing, politely but firmly. ‘A summary, Lee. Plcase.’

Lee relished the attention, of course, but finally obliged. 'As long as nothing goes wrong in France, you should be fine. The Good Samaritan Law will give you quite a lot of leeway,' He looked up, eyes glinting, but Alan had missed the pun. 'The English can't touch you if no action happens in UK waters. But if there's an accident – if anyone dies or claims harm – then French law will apply and you'll be liable.' He wagged a finger for emphasis. 'And whatever you do, don't open a bank account. Terror laws can be applied very widely. Assets frozen, questions asked. Bitcoin, Alan. Bitcoin is your friend.' He lowered his voice to a conspiratorial murmur, as though the hedgerows might be bugged.

Alan even let him win a hole or two, buttering him up, dropping a couple of shots so they were level by the 18th.

The next day he played an altogether more pleasant round with Colin. Where Alan's success was obvious – the Sunseeker moored at Ramsgate, the chain of pharmacies across England – Colin's was more mysterious. Electronics, components, some factories, exports. Who really knew what it all added up to?

Still, Alan decided to go first. On the 17th green, his favourite place to seal a deal, he came out with it: 'I'm willing to put up two million. That's forty percent if we run for nine months. It's better that than leaving it to the taxman when we're gone. Leslie and I have no children and I believe in Bill.'

Colin's turn. 'I can put in a million and ideally it would be a loan.' He hesitated, 'Though I'd like to know how on earth we'd get repaid.'

Alan shrugged. 'Honestly, I don't know.'

That might have been the end of it, but Colin smiled faintly. 'Lee says crypto, does he? That's not a problem at all. I've been dabbling for a while and I'll show you how to set up a wallet.'

They looked each other in the eye and shook hands. Three million between them. A loan on paper, though both knew the chances of repayment were slim. Before they would have expected someone else to fix this problem, but something must have changed, as now both of them wanted to give it a go. And with their own money.

That evening, the four men gathered at the bar. Bill and Dave were leaning on the counter when Alan and Colin walked in. Dave, first round in hand, was practically fizzing.

'Look lads. We need a name. We can't just be "the panel of experts." And *Coastal Defence League* is dull as ditchwater. But think – who we are, where we meet, what we're planning. I say we call ourselves *The Buccaneers*.'

They laughed at first, but Dave pressed on. 'A buccaneer was like a pirate, but one tolerated by the French and the English, because they mostly robbed Spanish galleons. They were free-spirited, independent-minded and bold. They were doing what the governments couldn't or wouldn't do.' Bill didn't need to hear anymore. Without hesitation he raised his glass: 'To the Buccaneers!'

After the toast, Alan and Colin shared their news: the legal risks were manageable, funding had materialised, Colin's crypto knowledge solved a practical headache. Spreadsheets were passed around and numbers sketched on the back of napkins.

Dave, pleased to have moved from the sidelines, unveiled a sketch logo he had mocked up. An old sailing ship inside a circle with 'Buccaneers' written round the bottom. If you squinted, the mast and sails looked suspiciously like a raised middle finger.

The men roared with laughter. 'Perfect,' Bill declared.

But amid the progress and the joking, Alan sounded a note of caution. 'Look, I can't move forward without Leslie's support. She's my conscience in life. You all know that.'

The others nodded. They agreed to raise the matter gently at the collective Christmas dinner in mid-December. Also, they put the St George's Carol Service in their diaries. The night ended, as ever, with bad jokes, complaints about the country and a round of muttering about 'Gary ruddy Lineker.' But beneath the banter, something had shifted. The Buccaneers had a name, a plan and the beginnings of a war chest.

When he got home Alan mentioned to Leslie that they were all going to come to the Carol Service. She was pleased but reminded Alan that he could come any Sunday.

'No, no,' Alan replied with mock horror. 'I couldn't join the God-botherers!'

Chapter 10
Silent Night, Distant Shores

Indiana in December had a way of biting through coats and scarves. The fields around Naylor were stripped bare and frosted at the edges. It was the kind of landscape that looked beautiful from indoors and felt brutal once you stepped outside. Micah teased Gabriella that it was a ‘good Texas breeze’, whenever she pulled her gloves higher over her wrists. She rolled her eyes and told him he had no idea what a real winter was.

At Naylor, the cold meant only one thing: preparations for the famous Silent Night basketball game. Every December, the students packed into the gym, waiting in complete silence until the tenth point was scored, at which moment the place erupted, a roar so loud it often made national news. Later they sang *Silent Night* unaccompanied. It was the tradition everyone secretly adored: part sport, part theatre, part communal joy. Gabriella was already working on her outfit with her roommates.

Meanwhile, classes had taken an unexpected turn. Gabriella had signed up for Public Relations almost on a whim but found herself thriving. The department had its own mock studio, complete with lights, green screen and microphones. Students took turns grilling each other with tough questions, learning the formula: Acknowledge. Deflect. Speak.

‘Let’s hear it, Gabriella,’ her tutor said, and she stepped into the lights. It turned out the camera loved her. Afterwards, a classmate joked, ‘I mean, in real life you’re pretty average, but on screen you’re a ten.’ Everyone laughed, Gabriella most of all. She was genuinely surprised and found it surreal, even amusing, that something as small as a lens could make her look so different. Micah took a different tack, teasing her that when she graduated she would work at Fox News.

Micah had started posting films about Naylor on TikTok. He’d always thought he took after his father, but now he saw how much of his mother’s theatrical streak had rubbed off. Creating one-minute dramas felt second nature – polished, playful, and always matched with the perfect soundtrack.

Between them, the weeks slid by – classes, chapel, late-night coffee runs, the first flurries of snow. And all the while, April in Deal felt far away. Then, just before they left, a letter arrived from England. It was a Christmas card, showing St George’s Church, its porch and roof dusted with snow, lanterns glowing in the windows. Inside was a handwritten note in the Vicar’s hard-to-read script:

‘At Christmas we remember how the old covenant gave way to the new; how the old world gave birth to the new. We hope and pray that Deal may hold a little of that Spirit for you both. We know you will bring something fresh to us, and we hope that you will also receive something deep and lasting in return. We can’t wait to welcome you in April. Happy Christmas!’

Gabriella read it twice, her expression softening. Micah turned the card over in his hands, tracing the outline of the church door. Neither said much, but both felt the same thing: the pull was growing stronger. England was no longer just an assignment. It was a place, waiting.

Chapter 11
Smuggling Routes

The false-floor truck rattled Abdul over the rough Afghan roads, carrying him toward the first of two borders. Each bump reminded him that this journey was neither simple nor safe. Zaranj disappeared behind him, its sun-baked streets fading into the horizon, leaving only the dust, the heat and the relentless rhythm of the tyres on the dirt track.

At the Afghan-Iran border, Abdul was kept hidden through the checkpoint. There were eyes everywhere, some curious, some indifferent. But he stayed still, breathed silently and wasn't discovered.

Once through, he was placed in another truck for the trek through Iran. The terrain shifted as dryness gave way to scrubland and then to mountains rising ahead in the distance. The vehicle was cramped but at least he was out of false floors for the moment. His fellow travellers spoke little, their faces set, their eyes scanning constantly. Abdul kept his mind occupied, reading maps in his head, rehearsing every step of what came next.

At the Iran-Turkey border, the tension ratcheted up. Security was tighter, the lines longer, the air thick with impatience. Abdul was placed in another false floor compartment, this time with seven other people. It was scary and claustrophobic. His pulse quickened through the border, but they held steady and made it through. At the next town the truck set them down, letting them make their own way through Turkey.

That night, sitting in a sparse safehouse, Abdul allowed himself a moment of reflection. He looked at the ceiling, tired but alert and whispered a prayer for his father, for the pharmacy, for the city that had raised him. The journey was not over, but he had survived two borders. And for the first time in months, the faintest glimmer of hope returned.

Chapter 12
From Advent to Anger

Alan had been mulling for weeks about how best to present his plans to Leslie. It wasn't that he was frightened of her; he'd never put it like that. But he knew she was sensible, grounded and allergic to anything that smacked of recklessness. The last thing he wanted was for her to think he was about to pour two million into a crazy vigilante caper. Yet that was the obvious conclusion a sensible wife might draw.

One Sunday evening, glass of wine in hand, Alan asked, as he often did, 'So what did the vicar say this morning?'

Leslie was folding napkins at the table. 'Well, it's Advent, so it was about the Second Coming. He was very good, actually. He asked us to think about what good we'd want to be found doing when Jesus returns and the world ends.'

Alan gave a half-smile. He'd never been sure about the Second Coming – even in his churchgoing days, it had always sounded rather far-fetched. 'Is there a screening of *The Omen* this week as well?' he joked, trying to deflect.

Leslie chuckled but pressed on. 'No, silly. The point was: what can we do now that we won't be able to do later?'

Well, he thought, that was as good an opening as he was going to get. So, Alan gently laid out a brief outline of the plan. He kept it simple, stripped back to the essentials. And he mentioned the figure – two million – because he knew Leslie hated it when costs were sprung on her later.

To her credit, she didn't explode. It was the first time Alan had ever raised anything so serious about the small boats; the idea of 'buccaneering' held no appeal. For a moment, she wondered if her husband had completely lost his senses. Still, she agreed to give it some thought, admitting that, yes, the country was in crisis.

Bill had no one at home to convince. Colin had a similar conversation with Miranda, who had to be told three times that this wasn't a joke. Dave's partner Laura was so tired with the school Nativity play that she just made a 'W' symbol at him.

Leslie's concerns grew and privately, without telling Alan, she arranged to see the Vicar. He welcomed her in, gave her tea and let her speak. In confidence, she shared Alan's plan and her worries: about legality, safety, costs and the danger of meddling where perhaps they shouldn't.

The Vicar listened patiently. He agreed that Christians should respect, indeed obey the God-given authorities of the land. With Christmas approaching, they also remembered that Jesus had once been a refugee in Egypt. Yet the body he had found on the beach stayed with him. He wondered aloud what a Christian should do when the authorities weren't doing their part. 'If you truly loved your neighbour as yourself,' he asked, 'would you really let them board one of those little boats?' He admitted he couldn't speak to the law, but morally, he felt the plan was finely balanced. In his experience, he added, 'people more often regret the things they don't try for the Lord than the things they do, even when they don't work out.'

Then he surprised her. 'Why don't we pray and ask God to guide you? Let's try a "fleece," like Gideon did when he wanted a clear sign. The fleece stayed dry while the ground around it became wet – that's how he knew. Why don't we do the same until the end of the year and see what God shows us?'

He prayed a beautiful, steadying prayer and Leslie left relieved, lighter and glad to have placed the whole thing into God's hands.

The Christmas dinner rolled around, a noisy and familiar occasion. The women were merciless with the banter. 'What's next, lads? A trip to the moon? Oh, hang on what's that in your pocket, Dave? A Nobel Peace Prize?!'

But over coffee, Leslie, often the moral barometer among them, repeated the Vicar's words. 'He said it's finely balanced morally. And he advised we ask for a sign.'

Bill bristled. 'A sign? How many more do we need? What's the point of fighting for King and country? What's the point of passports? Or having a navy if you won't use it? Isn't there a parable about doing the good we can do?'

Miranda, ever the peacemaker, tried to steady the ship. 'There is a case to act, Bill. But if it's the right thing, perhaps God will show us all in some way.'

Bill agreed but muttered about dithering politicians.

St George's went all out for Christmas. The Carol Service was candlelit, the flames spreading row by row from the Vicar's first taper at the front. The familiar carols rose, warm against the cold stone walls.

Alan, who hadn't been expecting much, found himself intrigued by the sermon. He had braced himself for climate change, wacky poems or 'Jesus the refugee'. Instead, the Vicar preached that faith, in his view, was spelt R-I-S-K. He listed all the risks God had taken in sending his baby son to the world. And then he posed a challenge for 2025: 'What risks might God be asking you to take in the New Year? What would faith look like for you if it was spelt R-I-S-K?'

Alan shifted in the pew. It struck uncomfortably close to home. Then came the notices. Alongside appeals for help with visits and Christmas hampers, the Vicar mentioned something unexpected: 'We're delighted to announce that two American helpers will be joining us next summer.'

Alan nearly choked. British God-botherers were one thing. But now Yanks as well? Why did we have to import all the worst things from America?

When Christmas itself came the Buccaneers all scattered to their own traditions. Alan and Leslie had Bill over, as they had for years. Colin and Miranda's house was alive with the laughter of returning children. Dave shuttled between Laura's family in the South and his own in the North, trying to be everywhere at once.

For a few days, the world slowed: crackers, port, old films on television. Then Boxing Day arrived.

With Christmas having fallen on a Thursday, the weekend stretched ahead, making Friday the perfect night for going out. It was like a national binge. Pubs were full, clubs spilling over, taxis crawling till dawn. But by Sunday morning, the country's mood had curdled.

In Bolton, Kelsey Norman went out but never made it home. Walking past a migrant hotel, she was attacked and killed. CCTV footage led police straight to her attacker: a man from Djibouti who had crossed the Channel illegally only weeks before.

Then came the second blow. The disappearance of Alice Sherborne in Norfolk transfixed the nation. A nineteen year old girl, studying History at Durham University, she had been staying with friends in the Burnhams. On Boxing Day night they had gone to the yacht club, staggering home across the marshes. Alice never arrived.

Her parents made desperate, tearful appeals, filmed on their lawn in Hampshire. Friends from school and University added their voices. By Monday evening, Alice's body was found sixty miles away in Lincolnshire. She had been sexually assaulted and then murdered, with DNA again pointing to a recent small boat arrival.

When the News at Ten revealed the link, the Buccaneers sat in silence. Leslie's face was pale in the glow of the television. She turned to Alan and said, slowly but firmly:

‘You have to go and stop this. These murders are terrible – those poor girls! No one knows who we are letting across.’

The nation seethed. For years governments had promised action. Now two young women were dead and the patience of people from all walks of life had run out. Prime Minister Starter looked dazed, still speaking the language of human rights while the public spoke the language of human fears.

Chapter 13
A German Christmas

Abdul had not expected to stay in Germany. Nuremberg was supposed to be a pause, a breath before the last push towards Calais. His cousin's house in a small village outside the city was crowded but warm and he imagined he would be gone in days. Yet one conversation changed everything.

The village pharmacy was desperate for staff over Christmas. Their assistant had broken her arm and the owner was swamped. Abdul's cousin let slip that he was a trained pharmacist. His German vocabulary was limited to 'Guten Tag' and 'Danke,' but his English was fluent and that was enough. Medicines had Latin names, patients could point and the rest he picked up fast.

To his surprise, they offered him proper pay. At the end of his first week, he calculated he would earn in a month what would have taken six back in Lashkargah. He was, briefly, a success story; a man who had crossed borders and found useful work.

But the shadow of the smugglers remained. He had paid to reach Turkey and as he'd made his way across Europe he had run down his savings. Now he would need to pay again, and more, if he wanted a place on one of the boats that crossed from France to England. His cousin reminded him of this bluntly: 'You can enjoy Germany, but you cannot stay. You are a guest of chance.'

On Christmas Eve, with the pharmacy closed, Abdul wandered through the city. Nuremberg's famous markets were still buzzing, even in the thin, cold air. Rows of stalls glowed with fairy lights; the air smelled of cinnamon, roasted nuts and sausages sizzling on griddles.

He walked slowly, hands in his pockets, watching families drift between the stalls. Children tugged at mittens, laughing at the carousel. Young couples held mugs of steaming Glühwein, their faces pink from the chill. Abdul felt no urge to drink or to join in, but he was moved all the same. It was not his festival, nor his faith. Yet he could not deny the sweetness of it: the small lights in the depth of winter, the way people carried themselves with a kind of joy, the sense of belonging to something larger. He felt, for the first time in months, the ache of loneliness.

He bought a small paper bag of sugared almonds and ate them slowly, one by one, before turning back towards the village. The smugglers would have to be paid. England still waited. But for one afternoon, under the glow of Christmas lanterns, Abdul allowed himself to feel at peace.

Chapter 14
The First Watch

The Buccaneers met again on the first Monday of January, pints in hand, but with little laughter. All agreed they had to act and with the decision made they now had eight weeks to prepare to be ready for March 1st. The Buccaneers were moving from planning to action.

Bill took the lead, his mind already racing. He wanted Ribs that looked ordinary but could fly: six metres long, fast enough to cover the twelve-mile dash from France in under fifteen minutes. Through Boatworld and old comrades, he found three suitable vessels. A Portsmouth yard began some 'modifications.' They were a subtle enough outfit to avoid too many questions.

Alan worked the yachting set, dropping hints over golf games and lunches. Volunteers began lining up for 'wine trips' to Boulogne.

Colin disappeared into his workshop, coaxing drones into life. Recon models with twenty minutes of flight, assault drones that could land, fire a bolt and puncture a dinghy in seconds. A few comic disasters – a greenhouse ruined, a startled terrier – but gradually, the prototypes began to work.

Dave became quartermaster, receiving a steady stream of branded kit, duffel bags and binoculars. He nudged camping friends toward 'birdwatching' weekends near Calais, offering reassurance with a grin when they asked too many questions.

Bill ran civilian training in the parish hall: map reading, pin-drops and code words hidden in a bird guide. 'Little tern' for a small Rib, 'greater tern' for a large one, 'albatross' for anything monstrous. They left a little steadier, laughter breaking through their nerves.

The veterans came too. Ray and Larry, old frogmen mates, joined a steady trickle of wiry men who found a welcome at The Royal Oak in Ramsgate. £400 a day bought commitment and discretion.

Alan signed cheques without blinking, pounds for now, but Colin showed him how to pay with bitcoin as well.

Leslie, meanwhile, asked the Vicar for guidance on how to pray for the project. A week later, he returned with a small card with Sir Francis Drake's words printed on both sides.

'Disturb us, Lord, when we have dreamed too little.'

Alan loved it and asked Leslie to order a set with enough for the whole team.

By late February, the Buccaneers numbered more than a hundred crew and volunteers. The church hall hosted a team building dinner. Alan gave a rousing speech, firm about no publicity, no social media, cover stories rehearsed.

As pudding was cleared, the Vicar appeared, looking for some PCC papers – but pressed to speak, he read Drake's prayer aloud:

'Disturb us, Lord, to dare more boldly,
To venture on wider seas
Where storms will show your mastery;
Where losing sight of land, we shall find the stars.
We ask You to push back the horizons of our hopes;
And to push into the future in strength, courage, hope
and love.'

The room hushed. Veterans, yachties, campers, engineers – all listened, each word finding its mark. Eyes flicked around the hall, the air almost vibrating with rising courage.

Bill broke the silence with a grin, lifting his glass.

'Amen to that. Let's go and do some serious disturbing.'

And so they did.

Everyone was ready to begin patrols on Sunday, March 1st. Leslie wasn't thrilled, as she'd wanted to go to church. In the end the weather prevailed: the rain and wind had eased by Saturday, but the swell stayed high on Sunday, rolling hard against the pier.

The team was full of tension. Colin checked and re-checked the drones, running batteries down and charging them again. Dave had everyone kitted out. Bill walked the quay before dawn, tested every outboard and ran through the brief twice. The first Scouts were already in France, having gone ahead through the Eurotunnel. The WhatsApp groups were ready to ping.

It was St David's Day and Leslie came home from church with a daffodil for Alan. Over a drink he asked what the vicar had spoken about.

'The life of St David,' she said. 'Apparently he lived in France for a while, he was a monk, he helped bring the good news to Wales, and he lived on leeks and water.'

Alan didn't look that inspired but nodded politely. His thoughts were already on the day ahead, turning over every possibility. He used to feel like that when he opened a new pharmacy, that familiar rush in the gut. This felt the same, only bigger.

At 3.30 am alarms sounded across East Kent. Lights blinked on in homes and B&Bs, cars and vans coughed into life. Down at Ramsgate Marina the first shapes gathered in the dark. A few lads had slept in rooms at the Royal Oak, so it was only a short stumble to the quay. Bill was already there, cap pulled low, clipboard in hand, ticking off names as the wind came off the water.

Three pleasure cruisers, one support ship and three Ribs were each crewed, fuelled and ready. They slipped their lines and nosed out into the black water. They weren't quite on autopilot, but everyone knew where they were heading. The cruisers made quickly for their sectors, covering roughly twenty miles of coastline each between Dunkirk and Boulogne. By five am they were in position, engines idling, drifting slowly toward Calais. The crew raised the recon drones, red lights winking against the dark sky.

At first there was nothing to see and no pings from the Scouts. Two Ribs held position at the international line, waiting like dogs on a leash. Bill pressed further, hugging the coast south of Cap Gris-Nez. He flashed his torch once, saw two flashes back, and waited. He hadn't seen Philippe for three years, not since their last expedition in the Gulf. 'The Eel', they'd called him back then, calm as ever.

A shadow rose out of the dark water and Philippe climbed aboard, dripping and grinning. Bill handed him a towel. The other French lads were capable enough, but Philippe was the one he trusted. If anything went wrong, Bill always knew Philippe could take over. They swung round and headed back to the mid Channel rendezvous.

The smugglers, meanwhile, had been watching the same forecasts. Monday morning looked perfect. A passage cost two thousand euros, sadly much less than it used to. Having said that the four men in the gang stood to make forty thousand euros by breakfast. The plan was routine: inflate the boat, fit the engines, load the fuel and passengers, and then vanish before dawn.

At Audresselles, a battered grey van rolled to a stop beside the little river. It reversed, opened its back doors and dropped a dinghy into the shallow water. Compressors hissed and within minutes the boat stood rigid, grey and gleaming. Two men bolted on the engine, another stacked jerry cans of fuel.

At five-thirty, thirty-six migrants appeared from the lanes and dunes, guided by their phones. They lined up quietly, reaching for the so-called lifejackets. There were only thirty. Someone asked if anyone could swim. No one answered.

Out to sea, a small Rib with two men pretended to fish; this was the pick-up crew, waiting to collect the smugglers once the run was done. Jean, the ringleader, had made dozens of crossings. He kept saying he'd retire after one more. But the money; he always needed a little bit more. What Jean didn't know was that he'd already been seen by the eye in the sky.

Southern sector's patrol drones had spotted the grey inflatable and marked the position. The 'greater tern' alert was sent out and Bill and Philippe pushed the throttle forward; fifteen minutes until contact.

Colin's puncture drones were already airborne, three of them tracking Jean's inflatable. The operators were cautious; migrants were milling around and they needed a clear moment. Then, as the boat was pushed down the river to the shore, it was suddenly all alone, bar the smugglers helping it along.

It was over in seconds.

Jean heard the whirr first, then saw three alien-like shapes dive. Three soft pops and air hissed from his boat like steam. The dinghy sagged, half-deflated before he could move. What was going on? Who was doing this? He grabbed a coat and smothered one drone, but the other two were up and away into the sky.

The recon drone stayed aloft, filming. Then the code went out – 'Drake' – a successful interception. There were cheers out in the Channel and in Ramsgate. Bill saw the message and allowed himself a brief nod of satisfaction. He eased back the throttle and as there was no need to be seen, they turned round and headed back.

When the first shift gathered at HQ later that day, the place was buzzing. Bill had found a shop on Harbour Street, wedged between a betting shop and Oxfam. He had picked it because the windows were painted white, so it looked empty and because there was an easy access door from the quay. He had a false wall built inside so that, from the High Street, it looked like an unused shop. But behind the wall the real work happened: maps, chargers, radios, lockers, a coffee machine that always hummed. Two people were on duty during shifts, coordinating the patrols.

Alan had even brought in an old wartime naval map he had bought at a charity auction. It had little magnetic ships you could push around the Channel. He'd sneaked it in after dark and now it hung on the wall, offering encouragement from an earlier era.

Every day, after each shift, they logged what they had done, seen and heard. And the first line in the ledger simply and proudly read:

'March 2nd – One successful interception.'

Chapter 15
Tennis Racket Chaos

The next day, no boats tried to leave. The Scouts watched their designated spots, but all remained still. The migrants wondered around their camps, frustrated and fearful; they just wanted to reach England and claim asylum; yet here they were, waiting, uncertain and nervous.

Jean wasn't stupid. That afternoon he went to Decathlon on the Calais ring road and bought twenty of the cheapest tennis rackets he could find.

The following morning, Colin and Laura were up before dawn, drones humming, batteries checked and double-checked. After a smooth Channel crossing, they launched their little machines into the pale light. Laura hunched over the feed.

'I swear, if I have to watch another empty beach, I'll start naming every pebble,' she said.

Colin grinned without looking up. 'That one's Gerald. Solid type. Been here since the Ice Age. And that's Maurice. Crumbles under pressure.'

'Sounds very much like half the lads at the golf club,' Laura shot back.

The laughter was brief but eased the tension. Then the feed jolted alive; shadows moving across three separate spots in the Southern sector.

'Contact,' Laura said sharply.

'Three groups, all leaving at once?' Colin leaned in. 'So, they've been talking.'

The recon drones stayed high scanning, while the puncture drones swept in. Two boats were stopped quickly; the third wobbled as figures on the beach swung something at the machines.

'Wait. Are they using tennis rackets?' Laura blinked.

They looked carefully at their HD feed and saw a chopping racket clip a drone, sending it tumbling into a whirl of sand and plastic.

Out at sea, Bill and Philippe powered toward Audresselles in their Rib, waiting for a 'Drake' message to confirm success. But unbeknown to them, the rackets were proving effective, and the grey inflatable was already being loaded.

Philippe, clad in al!-black swimwear with fins and hand extensions, looked every bit the special-forces operative. Knife strapped to one calf, slimline torch on the other. Through the binoculars he saw the inflatable: half-filled with figures clambering aboard. As Bill powered past, cool and composed, Philippe dove into the sea. A small air canister between his teeth kept him submerged. Bill didn't think he had been seen, a view that was about to be tested.

The lumbering eleven metre Rib from Jean's gang chugged off the beach. Philippe swam beneath it and drove his knife into the air tanks, carving a six-foot gash along the starboard side. Then, quick as a flash, he slashed the port tanks. The deflation and chaos sent twenty migrants into the sea; the rest clung on to the limping craft.

Philippe vanished, swimming a hundred metres out to sea before surfacing. He watched the horizon for Bill's return run North and signalled to him with his torch. Bill slowed, reached out and hauled him aboard. As they sped away, Philippe looked back through his binoculars: migrants cold, shivering and frightened were making for the beach. Jean, furious, was already wading in, dragging the boat ashore so he could retrieve the engine.

Elsewhere, another gang tried a different approach: a smaller, pre-inflated dinghy with seven migrants aboard. The recon drones caught it, but by the time the attack drones and Rib arrived it was out beyond the ferry lane and was unsafe to intercept.

Later that morning, at a roadside café on the edge of Calais, Jean and the others gathered over bitter coffee. They spoke in low voices.

'What just happened?' one hissed.

'There are drones,' Jean muttered. 'They're coming from somewhere and targeting the boats.'

'But we had everything planned!' another protested.

Jean rubbed his forehead, eyes darting. The devil had appeared, he thought, and they were powerless to stop him.

'Should we film them?' someone asked.

'Publicity's bad,' Jean snapped.

'Tell the police?'

'No,' said another. 'You forget – what we do is illegal.'

Jean exhaled, defeated. 'For now, let's use tennis rackets, until we find something better.'

That day was another triumph for the Buccaneers: three interceptions and only one small boat making it across.

Back at Ramsgate HQ, the logs were updated, mugs refilled, and spirits ran high. No one outside seemed to notice the extra traffic in and out of the marina. The smugglers' frustration only confirmed what the Buccaneers already knew; they were beginning to make a difference.

By the end of March, their cat-and-mouse game with the smugglers had become routine. Each day brought fresh tension and new challenges, yet the team had settled into a rhythm that worked. The monthly dinner at the bar was quite an event – stories shared, jokes cracked, and a quiet satisfaction running around the table that their mission was proving its worth.

Even the UK Border Force was starting to take notice. Only 106 migrants had made it across in March, a fraction of the few thousand expected. One officer, puzzled by the drop, spoke with his French counterpart. He replied that no complaints had been filed, but said enquiries would be made. The numbers were only published quarterly, so the impact of the Buccaneers' work wouldn't be seen officially until mid-April.

Over the Easter weekend, the weather broke. Leslie was inwardly relieved; the rain gave her an excuse to go to church in peace. Colin and Alan, meanwhile, pulled on their checked trousers and V-neck sweaters for a round of golf. Both agreed, without saying so, that this was some of the best money they had ever spent: camaraderie, exercise, purpose and the rare luxury of time to think.

As time wore on, the truth of what was happening in Deal and Ramsgate became an open secret. People sensed the unusual activity along the coast but, true to form, said nothing. These were towns that had long avoided authority for reasons both practical and stubborn; no one was going to question a few yachts and pleasure boats vanishing into the Channel.

On the Tuesday after Easter, the UK Border officer received a note from his French counterpart. Someone unknown, had apparently been 'interfering' and stopping the boats from launching. Details were sketchy and the message was brief: 'As long as no one gets hurt, it's best left alone.'

'Ruddy French,' the officer muttered, shaking his head. Yet, in truth, the line summed things up perfectly. The French wanted the migrants gone from Calais and didn't much care where they went.

But the problem was growing. Migrants were piling up along the coast, more desperate and frustrated with each failed attempt. Every delay fed the sense of urgency. Some wandered around aimlessly, others argued about their transport. Tensions simmered. The smugglers were becoming more inventive and reckless, but the Buccaneers were ready, vigilant and confident that, as long as they kept careful watch, they could stay one step ahead.

The game was changing and both sides knew it. Yet in the quiet moments – the calm before dawn, the clink of glasses in the bar, the flash of sunlight across the Channel – there was a strange thrill to the chase. The Buccaneers' impact was growing and they hoped it would remain their secret success.

Chapter 16
Crossing the Waters

Before leaving for England, Micah and Gabriella were summoned to meet President David and his wife, Sarah. The meeting was part pep talk, part cultural briefing and part prayer.

David and Sarah had spent a year in Cambridge, where they'd met the Vicar and his wife Kathryn, and spoke of England with a mixture of affection, pride and caution. President David leaned forward, his tone brisk but warm.

'Listen carefully. The mistake is to think Brits are just Americans in another time zone. They're not.'

Sarah added with a grin, 'They drink tea, a lot. Try it if you like but stash some soda just in case.'

Micah frowned. 'Tea, got it. Soda backup.'

'They speak more quietly,' David continued, 'and sometimes it's hard to tell what they really mean. They'll use four adjectives where we'd use one. And their sense of history; it seeps into everything.'

Gabriella listened closely. 'So, same language, but different culture?'

'Exactly,' Sarah said. 'And they drink more alcohol, and in more ways. Life there can be both more sophisticated and less, all at the same time. Their humour's sharp; sometimes it takes a while to tune in. Don't be intimidated.'

David leaned back. 'Remember, you're on a mission. The Vicar's a man of God I respect hugely. Follow his lead. Your enthusiasm will be a breath of fresh air. The locals may seem cynical and sarcastic, but that's often just a front for a deep loyalty. In case the obvious needs saying: no romances, please. Make Naylor proud. And enjoy your three months.'

Gabriella nodded slowly, realising her TV-based picture of England – *Miss Marple*, polite queues, endless cups of tea – was probably a little off.

Sarah finished with a prayer, 'Lord, we commit this venture to you. We pray for your guidance and protection, for boldness and trust along the way.'

When it was over, Micah and Gabriella felt both daunted and exhilarated. They were stepping into a world both familiar and strange. What would England really be like?

Before leaving, they checked in with their prayer triplets. Micah worried about whether people would understand his accent; Gabriella worried about feeling small in a town older than her own country. After final calls home, Gabriella's mother drove them to Indianapolis airport for their flight. The overnight leg to Dublin was tiring, but the connection to London Gatwick went smoothly.

At arrivals, the Vicar and Kathryn were waiting, waving little Union Jacks and Stars and Stripes. Gabriella's mother looked pleased; she knew her daughter was in good hands. Enjoy your week in England, she thought to herself and breathe a little.

The drive to Deal was an adventure in itself. Micah was alarmed by the speed of the car, its compact size, the unfamiliar European sedans and, above all, driving on the wrong side of the road. While Gabriella and her mother napped, he stayed wide awake, tense and slightly terrified. Noticing his unease, the Vicar explained.

'With forty times less land than the States, it may feel a bit cramped at first. And efficiency matters here: petrol's seven dollars a gallon, so every mile counts.'

Micah, who'd grown up near the oilfields of Texas, was intrigued. 'If the UK has its own oil, why does the petrol cost so much?'

'About seventy-five percent is tax,' the Vicar said. 'But you're asking the right questions.'

Kathryn enjoyed the politeness, privately pleased to be addressed as 'Ma'am.'

At the Vicarage, a five-bedroom Victorian house beside the church, Micah and Gabriella were shown to their rooms, with an extra bed added for Gabriella's mum. The smell of the salt air washed through the town. The place was pleasant, though the garden was a little wild and the house showed signs of wear. Both rooms looked out into Deal's narrow streets with the sea but a hundred yards away.

Lunch was quick and calm. Afterwards, the Vicar suggested a nap to help with the jetlag.

As they paused Micah and Gabriella felt the weight of the coming three months – and the responsibility of representing Naylor faithfully. But more than that, they felt ready.

***

Hundreds of miles east, another crossing was beginning.

Abdul had been so effective at the pharmacy that his German employers asked him to stay on until Easter. This suited him fine. He'd even picked up a few useful ideas from the Germans – clever product placement, efficient software programs – though the personal touch wasn't their strength. People came to love him, particularly the older customers. Even speaking in English, his care shone through his eyes.

By now, he had saved enough to make the next leg of his journey and even wire some funds home. His brother had advised him on the safest border crossing between Germany and France, one that allowed him to walk in and avoid detection by authorities. It was a fifteen mile trek through the Black Forest, but Abdul had always loved the mountains, and he relished the thought.

He took the train to Gamshurst as instructed, carrying his mini-inflatable boat. Reaching the Rhine, he inflated it and floated gingerly across, leaving the boat on the shore. From there, he made his way through the dense woods, finally reaching a road. A bus took him south to Strasbourg and just like that, he was in France.

Though Germany had been kind to him, the adventure was far from over. His family knew the next crossing would be the most dangerous part of his journey and their messages of 'God's speed' via WhatsApp bolstered his courage as he continued onward.

Chapter 17
The Meeting

It was a familiar rhythm in England: bad weather over the Easter weekend, clearing just in time for school to start. Parents had joked about it for years. Through the rest of April and May, a pattern settled in – fine weather midweek, rain and wind on Fridays and Saturdays. For the Buccaneers, that meant surprisingly predictable days off and Friday nights in the bar. Alan and Leslie could still enjoy their Sunday drinks in peace.

Bill was quietly pleased with how the mission was going. The civilians had held up better than he'd expected. It didn't bother him that he was the poorest of the Buccaneers, living in a semi-detached ex-council house in Deal's North End. The view of the sea was all he needed. He kept the place immaculate: perfect lawn, no flowers, just a flagpole in the corner. Every morning and evening, without fail, he raised and lowered the Union Jack.

No one asked too many questions about what Bill did. His neighbours, Joan and Arthur, cut his grass when they knew he was away. Arthur was a patriot through and through – whatever Bill was up to; he was sure he approved.

The first Saturday after Easter, Bill sat outside watching the clouds lift when he noticed a drone sweeping along the seafront. It hovered, moving back and forth near St George's. Bill didn't like surprises. He set off on foot to investigate, sticking to familiar lanes and ducking behind trees to avoid being caught on camera.

Eventually, he spotted the operators on the pier – two young faces, not locals. One wore a jacket that read Naylor College, Indiana. Bill raised an eyebrow. They looked like Americans. But why were they filming in his town?

He intended to approach quietly, but they spotted him first and smiled. He relaxed and walked over.

'What are you two up to?' he asked.

The young woman spoke first, her accent smooth and distinctly Midwestern. They introduced themselves as Gabriella and Micah, placement students at St George's, filming a promotional video for the church website. Bill shook hands with each, feeling an unexpected ease.

Later, Micah would say he could tell Bill had a military background from the start. Gabriella, though, had no idea how pivotal that chance meeting would become.

'Have you ever been to the States, Mr Bill, Sir?' Micah asked eagerly.

Bill replied, 'I've worked with Americans a few times, yes. Navy.'

Micah's face lit up. 'No way! My brothers are in the Marines. Maybe you've met them?'

'I've not been with them for a few years,' Bill said honestly. He could read people well – it was part of his training – and he liked these two. Straightforward, good manners, open faces.

'When's the video going live?' he asked.

'The Vicar wants it up online on Monday,' said Gabriella. 'Before our first school visit.' She was doing the voiceover; Micah was in charge of the visuals.

Bill nodded. 'Alright. Just keep my house out of it please; I'm up the North End with the flagpole.'

'Yes, Sir,' said Micah, grinning.

Gabriella tilted her head. 'Do you come to St George's often?' Bill looked away briefly. 'I go for the Carol Service,' he said. 'If you meet Leslie Jones, I'm a friend of her husband, Alan.'

‘Well, do come back again,’ Gabriella said brightly.

‘And are you still serving, Mr Bill, Sir?’ Micah asked, hoping for a ‘yes’ to impress his brothers.

‘Am I still serving? Or am I retired?’ Bill asked himself rhetorically. ‘Technically I’m retired.’ He smiled and said his goodbyes.

The welcome service for Micah and Gabriella went well. They’d finished the promotional video early, so it was shown on Sunday morning. The Vicar hadn’t seen it beforehand as it was only finished just before the service. Gabriella and Micah found the congregation’s silence a little unsettling. But the pause was admiration, not indifference.

At ninety seconds, the video was brief but powerful. The aerial drone footage made Deal look magnificent; the pacing was cinematic. Yet it was Gabriella’s voiceover: warm, clear and gently reverent that elevated it. The Vicar recognised instantly that they had struck gold with these two and led the final hymn with gusto.

That evening, Leslie told Alan about the new arrivals and their film. He didn’t watch it but was pleased to hear that the church was trying something new.

By Monday morning, the swell had dropped again. Alarms were set for 3.30 am and the mission resumed. Deal returned to its quiet rhythm, the life of the town subtly pulsing around the determined vigilance of the Buccaneers.

Chapter 18
The Numbers Game

Wednesday April 8th marked the start of another chapter for the Buccaneers, though not on the water. Out in the Channel, things continued smoothly. The real storm broke on land when, that morning, the government released the first-quarter figures for small-boat crossings.

At the *Daily Mail*, staff practically salivated at the chance to hammer the government. Over at *The Guardian*, editors were already drafting their defences and deflections. Their nothingburger line had been well used and could probably be wheeled out one more time.

When the Home Office uploaded the official spreadsheet at 10 am, the reaction was universal disbelief. Numbers had been low through the winter, which was fair enough given the weather. But from March 1st, the graph appeared to plunge off a cliff. Officially, there had been only 106 arrivals that month: down 65% on February and a staggering 95% on March, the previous year.

Something was off. Officials had noticed, but the Easter break had delayed any attempt to find an explanation. By 10.03, the Home Office press phones were melting. Even the most cynical reporters hate being lied to and everyone sensed these figures couldn't be right.

The Home Office held the line, repeating the same numbers with no new explanation. *The Guardian* longed to claim the government's policies were working but couldn't point to a single change that might explain the drop. *The Mail*, meanwhile, should have been delighted as the boats had stopped! Yet, in their scepticism, they wanted to know how. Their editor barked orders across the newsroom:

‘I want to know if Dover’s processing centre is empty – properly empty. Are the RNLI and Border Force backing these numbers? I want someone on the French coast – have the migrants vanished? And if these figures are real, can someone please tell me how and why? I can’t print good news without answers; our readers won’t buy it.’ By lunchtime, Mail reporters were en route to Dover, Calais and using every phone contact they had.

The BBC, with its government sources, fared a little better. A single second-hand report from the French coastguard hinted at some ‘interference.’ But what? Lightning? Sharks? No one knew.

The Home Secretary sensibly sent a junior minister to defend the numbers in the Commons the next morning. There are only so many times one can say, ‘I don’t know,’ before looking daft.

By early afternoon, most outlets were forced to go with the same baffled headline: ‘The Mysteries of March – Channel Crossings Drop 95%.’

At *The Sun*, military sources whispered of ‘technical and Navy lads’ being drafted into some new job out of Ramsgate. Two reporters were dispatched immediately to find out more.

By evening, the Buccaneers were uneasy. They were used to rough seas, not the rougher ride of the British press. Over drinks at the bar, they laid it out.

‘How long do we have?’

‘Less than twenty-four hours.’

‘Who’s handling PR?’

Silence.

Dave was the only one sounding upbeat. ‘If the smugglers have a propaganda wing, we’ll need one too,’ he said. ‘Every battle has a media front.’

Then Bill's phone pinged with a WhatsApp message from Gabriella. She said she'd got his number from Leslie at church and wanted check the video was okay. Had it missed off his house? Dave hit 'play' on the small screen. 'Look lads, even the church is getting into PR!'

They leaned in, half-teasing, half-intrigued. Deal looked radiant, with sleek drone shots and warm narration. 'I really wouldn't mind living there,' quipped Colin. The Channel positively glowed as the light shimmered on the water. At the end, the Buccaneers fell silent.

'Could the Yanks do our PR?' Alan asked in a low voice.

Bill's phone pinged again. He read the message:

'The Vicar thinks you might be needing some PR help. Can we be of assistance?'

That afternoon, the Vicar had been uneasy. The media storm was coming and he had prayed for help. Leslie, at the earlier midweek communion, had voiced her own concerns. He'd hesitated to recommend Gabriella and Micah, though it was plain to him that the pair had been sent to Deal for more than school visits. Over tea, he asked gently about their communications experience.

Gabriella explained her Naylor media training – hostile interviews, crisis messaging, tone control. Micah spoke of his mother's influence as an actress, the film school and the discipline of storytelling. When pressed on rigour, Gabriella smiled. 'They train us to stay calm under fire,' she said.

The Vicar told them, in confidence, who the Buccaneers were and what they'd been doing. It was unconventional, he admitted, but he felt their mission was an answer to prayer. Gabriella and Micah had noticed the table at the back of St George's dedicated to missing migrants. There was an electric tealight and a name next to every soul lost in the English Channel.

The Vicar shared the story of pulling Maryam Ali's body from the sea. They agreed to reach out discreetly, just to test the waters. And so Gabriella messaged Bill.

While the Buccaneers went to bed anxious, Gabriella and Micah were wired with excitement. Gabriella's mother had flown home after a wonderful week exploring London and Canterbury. Her daughter was now properly on her own – flying the nest, as she put it, all part of the Lighthouse plan.

The next morning's patrol went as usual, but when the boats returned at 3 pm, the press were waiting. Alan, tired and hungry, found himself ambushed at the quayside. He did his best, remembering the phrase 'Citizens' Initiative', but fatigue betrayed him. Phrases like 'bloody foreigners' and 'useless government' slipped out. His passion came through, but also a strong resemblance to the reactionary Colonel Blimp. The one good thing was he deflected attention from the other boats.

The next day's headlines were merciless:

'Dad's Army on Patrol!'

'Racists in the Channel!'

'Golf Club Vigilantes!'

When he got home, Leslie met him at the door.

'I've just been doorstepped, dear.'

'Yes, I know. You're all over the news.' Online and TV news didn't have to wait until the morning. 'The BBC's called us vigilantes and the PM's said people mustn't take the law into their own hands.'

Alan dropped into a chair.

'How are you so calm?'

She poured him a drink. 'Eat first, then I'll explain.'

By six thirty, with food and wine restoring him Leslie let Alan in on the plan. The Beach, en route to Walmer, is the grandest street in town, where both Alan and Colin lived.

The doorbell rang, Alan's electric gates swung open and up the drive walked Gabriella and Micah.

Alan opened the door. Micah grinned. 'Pleased to meet you, Mr Alan, Sir!' Gabriella smiled and shook his hand.

Alan had always been discerning and even in his exhaustion, he sensed something solid in them. In a rare act of humility, he said simply:

'I'm struggling here. Can you rescue me?'

It broke the tension. They laughed and moved inside to the kitchen. Over a drink, Gabriella laid out what she'd prepared: a concise, confident plan. The first page read: 'Crisis Management.'

Alan winced. 'Good Lord. Is it that bad?'

'Today and tomorrow will be brutal,' Gabriella said, 'but after that it will get better.'

The next pages: 'Deflect and Explain.' Followed by 'Embed and Humanise.'

Alan excused himself, took the folder to the balcony, and called Colin. They spoke quickly and both agreed it couldn't get any worse than today. Both had experience of hiring young people who had excelled. If it worked with the Americans, great. If not, it would buy them time to find a professional firm from London.

Alan returned inside and said, 'Right. I've talked to Colin. We'll tell the others. If you want to go ahead tomorrow, call the press conference for five pm.'

Gabriella felt calm; Micah whooped. He wanted to review the recon drone footage straight away and join the early patrol for fresh video.

Gabriella's task was simpler: find the perfect backdrop. Something that spoke volumes before she said a word.

They left, buoyed and nervous in equal measure, each messaging their prayer triplets before bed. Tomorrow, the battle would be fought not at sea, but on camera.

Chapter 19
The Buccaneers Speak

Micah rose early with the Buccaneers at 3.30 am, eyes bright despite the chill. The dawn washed pink light over the Channel and through his drone lens he captured thrilling footage of the Ribs cutting across the water. Silvery spray flew up in the low light, engines humming like hornets. By the time they returned to the harbour, he was grinning like a cat who had got the cream.

At 8 am Gabriella pressed send on her first official release from Buccaneer Media. Short, direct and on point:

'There will be a press conference at 5 pm in front of the Maritime Museum in Ramsgate Harbour.'

The logo on the release was simple but bold. Dave had designed it weeks earlier, then tweaked it overnight so it looked more like a ship and less like a middle finger. By mid-morning, journalists' phones were humming.

The day was spent preparing. Gabriella sat at a long table upstairs at HQ, legal pad and coffee beside her. She ran through every line with the Buccaneers. Colin and Bill would flank her at the lectern, ready to field technical questions if pressed. But the core would be hers: framing their mission, shaping the story.

They agreed on their key messages:

- A concerned citizens' initiative
- Preventing boats from leaving France
- Safer for migrants, safer for Britain
- Daily updates with statistics
- Operational details withheld to protect interventions.

She worked the phrasing and polished the tone. The others listened as though she were briefing troops. Even Alan nodded. By four-thirty, they were all in position.

The evening was golden with a clean spring light casting long shadows across the harbour. The Museum sat proudly on a promontory, a handsome building pointing to the past. Facing the town, one could take in the full sweep of Ramsgate and its harbour. Dave had arranged for a lectern with the Buccaneer logo on to be placed on the quay, with one microphone feeding all the others.

The crowd of journalists was bigger than anyone expected. Cameras stacked in rows between the museum and the quay. Notebooks poised. A few locals wandered around curiously. The Buccaneers shifted uneasily at the edge, unused to being centre stage.

Gabriella stepped up. She stood straight, hair pinned back, notes neatly held. Her voice was calm, firm and deliberate.

'Good evening. The Buccaneers are a group of citizens, four men and their families, deeply concerned about the small boats in the Channel. Our concerns are simple: safety for the migrants attempting the crossing and safety for the people of the United Kingdom. These journeys are a danger to life and break the law. Using unconventional means, we disrupt the small boats before they leave France, safely stopping the crossings.

We began our initiative on March 1st. In the twenty-nine days since, we have patrolled the Channel and intercepted 113 craft. We estimate that 4,750 people have been prevented from making this dangerous journey.

We are not the government, a business, or a charity. We are concerned citizens, taking action where it has been lacking. Thank you.'

No one expected an American accent, but in this instance it lent credibility. It was an assured forty seconds, instantly picked up as a soundbite nationwide.

Flashbulbs snapped. Questions flew.

‘What’s your name?’

‘The Buccaneers,’ she said proudly.

‘Who funds you?’

‘The Buccaneers are self-funded,’ she replied smoothly.

‘Are you racist?’

‘No. The crossings are not safe and not legal, for all and any race.’

‘How do you do it?’

‘I cannot give operational details. To do so would endanger our work.’

‘How many people are involved?’

‘We are a mixture of staff and volunteers. At present our number is around one hundred.’

‘Is this legal?’

Gabriella met the question head-on:

‘In the United Kingdom, yes. No intervention takes place in UK territorial waters, so we remain compliant with British law. In France, the legal advice is clear: what we are doing falls within established Good Samaritan provisions. We intervene at the point where individuals are about to undertake a life-threatening journey, and under French law, that creates both a right and, arguably, a duty to act. We are confident our position is lawful.’

The press shouted over one another until Gabriella raised her hand.

‘One last thing. To ensure transparency, we will give daily updates. Tomorrow we will launch our new Instagram account: @BuccaneersUK, where footage and information will be shared directly. The first clip goes live tomorrow morning.’ Micah, just behind the cameras, had the 45-second highlight reel already cut: Ribs slicing across the dawn, spray catching the light. But Gabriella knew to pace the news; a steady drip, day by day, was how to keep the press hooked.

Finally, she closed her folder.

‘Thank you. We will meet you here again tomorrow at 5 pm. God bless Kent and God bless the United Kingdom.’

She stepped back. For a long moment, the journalists hesitated. They had come loaded for a fight but found themselves oddly disarmed. The facts were concrete, the delivery calm, the message unshakably human. Cameras still whirred, but the tone was shifting.

On the far side of the crowd, Deal’s MP Randy Hooger stood quietly, hands in his pockets, watching. He neither approached nor spoke, but his eyes narrowed with interest.

The Buccaneers exhaled as one. Their first skirmish with the press was over. They hadn’t sunk. They hadn’t even wobbled. Thanks to Gabriella, they might just have set sail.

The following day’s press was better, if a little mixed. The *Daily Mail’s* leader spoke for the media: ‘At least someone is doing something.’

The lunchtime phone-ins told a different story. Support for the Buccaneers was overwhelming and from all walks of life. One caller rang Jerry Klein approvingly, trying to play the National Anthem in the background as they spoke.

The Sun spotted a trend and decided to start a daily tally: Buccaneers vs Migrants. True to form, they added a third column: ‘Politicians,’ whose score began at zero.

Chapter 20
Ghosts of the Channel

Abdul's journey through France had gone more smoothly than he had dared to hope. By early April, after trains, buses and long stretches on foot, he finally reached Calais. He texted the number his brother had given him and soon met up with Jean's son, Pierre. He was wiry and self-possessed, with sharp eyes that missed nothing. He didn't waste time with pleasantries.

'You have the money?'

Abdul produced the bundle of euros – two thousand in notes he had counted and recounted on the way. Jean flicked through them quickly, satisfied, then gave a curt nod.

'Good. You'll get your place. But you'll have to wait. Maybe a few days, maybe longer.'

Abdul frowned. 'Why the wait? I thought boats went every day.'

Pierre's smile was thin. 'Normally, yes. But there's... interference. Engines failing, launches stopped before they reach the water. No one knows who or what, but it's making people nervous. I don't rush when the sea is restless and I don't rush when the ground is restless either. Understand?'

Abdul nodded, though unease prickled at him. Pierre seemed unbothered, even confident, like a man who believed he could weather any storm. 'You'll hear from me on WhatsApp when it's time. Until then – wait. Patience is part of the journey.'

And so Abdul found himself in one of the makeshift camps outside Calais. Plastic sheeting, wooden pallets, smoke from small fires – it was a place of waiting, of hushed conversations and restless eyes always turned toward the coast. It was here, in the evenings, that he began to hear the rumours. Whispered among Syrians, Afghans and Eritreans alike. Stories of English boats, fast and unseen, spoiling the crossings. Some called them fishermen, some said they were soldiers, others swore they were the ghosts of the Channel.

Abdul listened, saying little. He had learned in Germany the value of patience and silence. But the rumours stayed with him and when the wind carried the salt smell of the sea through the camp at night, he wondered if these mysterious Englishmen were the reason Pierre's 'few days' might stretch much longer.

Chapter 21
The Guardian Angel

For the rest of April the Buccaneers carried on, now very much in public. The establishment didn't know what to make of them. For years, the British had done what the man in the ministry said. Now the man in the ministry wasn't doing anything, citizens were taking over. The public, by and large, approved.

Micah worked with Bill to show as much as he could on film, without revealing tactics. Often this meant fast boats, men in shades and a bass that made windows tremble. But he also told the less flashy stories. Each day's stop was turned into a short, sharp film – with no aerial shots and no mention of campervans. The puncture drones were already well known and he captured a moment of chaos as a smuggler's boat was swarmed like a hive of bees. He was careful with the edit; less fear and more frustration and it landed perfectly.

Across the Channel, the pressure built. The Prime Minister, though privately appalled by 'citizen initiatives,' had the sense to say nothing. The French President was asked about the Buccaneers and responded with a shrug that said everything and nothing at once. Clearly, they hoped the matter would blow over.

Randy Hooger, Renew MP for Deal, met the Vicar for coffee. They knew each other well. The Vicar spoke of the body on the beach and said again that he felt the Buccaneers were an answer to prayer. Randy promised to stay in touch, though he knew he had to tread carefully.

Most politicians didn't know what to say. Criticise the Buccaneers and you looked petty; stay silent and you looked weak and indecisive. Full-on support was out of the question on either side of the Channel; it risked upsetting the opposing nation.

Still, the Buccaneers plan was working. Calais was filling up and Jean could barely get a boat away. One of the Ribs had been refitted with spikes around the prow; something between a jet-ski and a medieval battering ram. Bill and the crew tried to hit the boats fast enough to burst them, but not hard enough to harm anyone. There were close calls and capsizes, but the numbers were on their side.

The four-day-a-week press conferences had become a kind of cheerful echo of the old COVID briefings. People liked the numbers: green for crossings stopped (always climbing) and red for crossings made (always small). *The Sun* persisted in keeping its third column for 'Politicians' (always zero).

The press wanted more and Gabriella knew they were moving into the 'embed and humanise' phase. She agreed to let selected journalists go out with the Buccaneers. Bill didn't mind as he'd worked with embedded reporters before. He laid down one rule: 'They'll need iron guts,' he said. 'We can't have civvies puking while we're on manoeuvres.'

In early May, *The Guardian* sent Helen David down with a photographer called Chris. Helen had grown up on boats and, though sceptical, she recognised a story worth chasing.

They were told to report to Ramsgate Harbour at 3.30 am. As she later wrote: 'Men with short hair appeared out of the night like moths drawn to a lamp.' She contrasted them with 'the bickering middle-class couple putting their yacht at the nation's behest.'

They met Bill – 'going for a 1990s PT instructor look,' she wrote: 'black shorts with side slits and a fleece with the Buccaneer logo'. It built the scene nicely. But nothing prepared her or Chris for Philippe.

Bill went through the same routine he had every morning, but for Helen and Chris it was their first time. As they slowed by the beach, she noticed Philippe first: 'jet-black, wavy hair and square jaw striding down the beach' and then, without warning, he reached for the bottom of his hoodie and lifted it up over his head. At the first glimpse of his washboard stomach, Helen felt, for her readers' sake, that she should watch more closely.

'Are you getting this?' she asked Chris.

'Oh yes, sweetie,' he replied, glued to his viewfinder.

They were running a little later than usual – Bill didn't want to kill the civilians on their first trip – so the sun was rising behind the beach. Pink light spilled through gaps in the clouds. For the photographer, it was perfection.

In a way that later made her feel faintly ashamed, Helen found herself wishing Philippe would take off his trousers next. Instead, he folded his hoodie neatly behind him – nice back, strong shoulders she noted – and then 'his tracksuit bottoms came smoothly down revealing black French swimming trunks'. She chose the word 'revealing' deliberately and for once was grateful for France's 'no board shorts' law.

Philippe was blissfully unaware of the attention. He strode into the surf – a reverse Daniel Craig – water breaking against his thighs. Chris prayed he'd remembered to slot in the new SD card; this was way better than any fashion shoot.

Philippe powered out to the Rib and climbed aboard. He grinned at Bill and extended a dripping hand to Helen and Chris, his 'Bonjour' deep and unmistakably Gallic. Helen managed a weak, 'Pleased to meet you,' while Chris could only murmur, 'Bonjour,' à la Kenneth Williams.

Every day Bill handed Philippe a towel, but today Philippe had an audience. He dried himself off slowly, unhurried, the early sun catching the spray in his hair. Helen later wrote she had to keep pinching herself to believe any of this was real.

As they sped towards international waters, Bill stood rock-solid at the controls, while Philippe moved with the rhythm of the waves, muscles tightening and relaxing in time with the sea. When Bill finally cut the engine, Philippe accepted a mug of tea, pretending to like it. Then they began chatting with the civvies.

Helen learned that Philippe was an orphan from Lyon. His parents had been killed in Algeria, fighting for France. He'd joined up at sixteen and served twenty years, now working occasionally for friends like Bill. He lived mostly alone in a Volkswagen campervan.

They argued amiably as Helen pushed him on the legality and morality of their actions. Philippe parried with charm and reason. When she quoted international law, he smiled and quoted Proust: 'The real voyage of discovery consists not in seeking new landscapes, but in having new eyes.' In that instant, her mind was made up. If there was one Buccaneer *The Guardian* would support, it was Philippe.

Bill's phone pinged: 'Strap in. We're on.'

Helen and Chris tightened their seatbelts as the Rib surged forward, hitting fifty miles per hour. Philippe disappeared behind them, then re-emerged clad in black – knives and torches strapped to his body, goggles, fins, and a small air canister between his teeth.

It wasn't strictly necessary to dive backwards from a speeding Rib, but it made quite the show.

Bill handed Helen the binoculars and explained Philippe's objective. She watched as a submerged shadow approached a huge grey inflatable lumbering in the surf; it was packed with migrants. Then, in a flash, the boat deflated, Philippe's dagger plunging into its belly. People fell into the shallows, but they could wade safely to shore.

Helen was shaken by what she saw – the numbers aboard, the percentage of women, the lack of lifejackets, the sheer fragility of it all.

When Philippe reappeared offshore, panting, he fist-bumped Bill, another mission complete. The dawn sky behind them blushed pink.

Back in Deal, Helen wrote up her story. Any piece that begins: 'As a happy, newly married woman, I was surprised by…' was destined to go far. The photograph of Philippe stretching, half-lit and effortless, made the front page.

Helen and Chris were disappointed that only two pictures were used. But when she got back to London, her editor explained the plan. The story was generating huge traffic; Philippe's image in particular had gone viral. They would stretch this out: 'Fourteen Days of Philippe,' with a couple of photos released each day.

The French Buccaneer who saved lives and quoted Proust was a perfect storm: sexy, moral, mysterious. Older women were suddenly explaining to younger colleagues what a 'Diet Coke break' was. Philippe was a sensation and the Buccaneers were beginning to turn the PR war.

Chapter 22
The President Takes Note

President Ronald Pump liked to start his mornings in Washington by keeping in touch with his base and watching television. He often said he was sorry other politicians couldn't see the benefit. 'Television is power,' he'd remark, 'And I'm very good at it.'

As he came down the stairs from the residence, he spotted his granddaughter Tai and press Secretary Carolyn Nevis giggling over a phone.

'What's funny today?' he asked, smiling that grin that could charm or chill, depending on the lighting.

'Nothing, Grandpa. Absolutely nothing at all.'

'Show me,' said the President, voice dropping to that slightly dangerous register.

Tai surrendered. 'There's this group of English and French people in the Channel stopping migrant boats. The footage is… well… it's hot!' She scrolled and held up the phone. 'They're all over TikTok.'

On screen, a Rib pounded across grey water, drone footage circling as Philippe flexed at the prow, sea spray sparkling like diamonds. Tai tried not to stop giggling.

Pump handed the phone back, expression unreadable. 'How come I haven't heard of these guys?'

Just then Lucy Miles, his Chief of Staff, appeared.

'Lucy,' he said, 'Are you in on this Buccaneer thing?'

She smiled. 'Oh, I'm all in for Bill. Solid. Dependable. Legs like tree trunks.' Pump raised an eyebrow. 'Should I be truthing about this?'

Carolyn and Lucy exchanged a glance, then answered with practised nonchalance. 'Sure, if you like.'

They knew him too well. Encourage him too hard and he'd resist; pretend it didn't matter and he'd sense the game. Better to be casual and positive and hope he'd move onto something else.

This wasn't President Pump's first rodeo and he knew when he was being played. His eyes narrowed as the two women left: 'I'm definitely being handled. But why?'

In the Oval Office, he closed the door, pulled out his phone and searched for himself. Within seconds he saw it all: wall-to-wall coverage in Britain. A migrant story, men of action, a touch of danger. They even played golf. Why had this been kept from him?

He picked up the phone. 'Get me the British Prime Minister please.'

A minute later came the nasal tones of Sir Piers Starter, full of forced cheer. 'Ronald! How are you?!'

Pump cut straight to it. 'Looking forward to the World Cup. May the best team win.'

'Of course,' said the PM, laughing too hard.

'And tell me,' Pump went on, casual as a knife sliding into a sheath, 'What's this I hear about these Buccaneers?'

Sir Piers' heart sank. The plan to keep it off the President's radar had lasted longer than he'd dared hope. But now it was exposed. 'Oh, it's just a group of vigilantes,' he said, 'trying to solve what is really a very complex international legal problem.'

Pump bristled at that. 'I see U.S. nationals among them. My kind of people. Not vigilantes – concerned citizens. I'm thinking of truthing some support. This is our issue, isn't it?'

Would Sir Piers dare echo the "our"? He tried the diplomatic route: 'Mr President, of course you're free to truth as you wish. But as an ally, may I beg you – please hold off. At least until the World Cup's over. We wouldn't want to distract from the football, would we?' He finished with a nervous laugh.

Pump paused. 'No promises. But for you, I'll try. Good to talk, Piers.' The line went dead.

He buzzed for Lucy. 'Tell me everything. Exactly what's been going on. I want the full picture.'

She didn't sugar-coat it. Three weeks earlier, the PM had called asking the White House to dampen the story down – 'don't add fuel to the fire.'

Pump admired that. The Brits always did subtlety better than sincerity. And he liked Piers, in his way.

'Okay,' he said finally. 'No official support. Not yet. But if things change, they change.'

When Lucy left, he leaned back in his chair, mind ticking like a safe being cracked. He had a nose for deals and this one smelled promising.

He buzzed again. 'Get me the Attorney General. And someone who knows maritime, UK and French law. Keep it quiet. Say it's about a treaty or something.'

The outline of opportunity was hazy, but it always started that way. He could feel it already: something big taking shape, just below the surface.

Chapter 23
The Fever Breaks Out

June was a glorious month in England. The weather stayed fine, and the Buccaneers enjoyed being out on the water. Crossing attempts dipped, Calais seemed calmer, and the PR offensive surged.

One of Dave's old friends, Graham Dixon, worked at the clothing chain Primark. He got in touch to see if they could trial some branded Buccaneer gear. Finally, something Dave could own! He raised it with the Panel at the bar that Friday. Colin, Alan and Bill were utterly consumed with keeping their vice-grip on the small boats, so they gave it little thought. Dave mentioned revenues, floated the idea of a business bank account and everyone nodded it through. By the second pint, they were debating the World Cup, due to kick off shortly in America.

Across the Channel, Jean gathered the gang leaders in a greasy spoon on the outskirts of Calais. He wanted to know how many places they had sold all together. Between them, 4,500 migrants had paid, but hardly any boats had made it off the shore. Only the quick 'six-passenger runs' were slipping through. Jean leaned back, calm but sharp.

'This was always meant to be easy money,' he said. 'And I don't like to lose.'

He proposed a counterattack: no new bookings for now but prepare to launch all 4,500 in one massive push. 'Early July – perhaps the 9th or the 14th,' he added cryptically. The others, sensing he had a plan, fell into line.

Back in England, Primark's trial run of Buccaneer merchandise sold out within a morning. Everything except Philippe's trunks, which British men flatly refused to wear.

Graham, a seasoned buyer, hadn't seen anything like it since the Spice Girls. He persuaded the board to approve a huge order: five million items, the biggest in years.

Fast fashion worked its magic. Trucks from Turkey and Romania were unloading within days. Soon warehouses brimmed with Buccaneer tracksuits, shorts with side slits, water bottles, lunch boxes and hoodies – even Philippe's trunks, discreetly rebranded as underwear. A promotion with *The Sun* – 'Collect ten tokens, get a free Buccaneer bag!' – sent footfall through the roof. By the first Saturday of June, Primark had queues like Christmas Eve. Reports of shoppers scrapping over kit only fed the frenzy.

What swept Britain that June could only be called a fever. Not since Beatlemania had anything like this gripped the public. Bill had to draft in extra port security just to get the crew away on time. More than a thousand girls ditched their post-exam holidays to mount 'Find Philippe' tours in Northern France. Sometimes they found him on his early swims, fainting at the sight. Headteachers began recommending Ibiza as a safer alternative.

Quintin Betts of *The Mail* accused *The Guardian* of selling out, dubbing their coverage 'The Phwoarteen Days of Philippe.' Even the Vicar was swept up, caught praying with his dog on the beach. Doorstepped, he admitted he'd been reciting St Francis's Prayer for over two years. Overnight he became the 'spiritual Svengali' behind the 'Channel bandits.'

Marks & Spencer noticed that Primark's range included checked golfing trousers, a product line they had owned decades earlier. It took less than a week to dust off the old patterns, update them and get them into production. As Primark had the Buccaneer branding locked up, all Marks could do was place golf trousers and V-necks beside signs hailing 'The Buccaneering Spirit.' The public got it instantly and middle-class men flocked to emulate Alan and Colin's golf club chic.

The Mirror spotted that there was a Buccaneer for every occasion and ran a Saturday pull-out where readers could cut out and keep their favourite Buck. Gabriella looked demure, Micah fiddled with electronics, Philippe wore very little, Bill stood firm at the helm in his shorts. Colin posed in his factory, Alan in golf gear and Dave had a pint in hand, beaming Geordie-style.

One of the strangest side effects was the revival of the 90s PT instructor look. Where Londoners once sported tight, pastel coloured, cotton shorts, this summer it was black nylon Reebok-style numbers with deep side slits. On weekend mornings the capital teemed with them.

There was something about the sheer masculine presence of the Bucks protecting the country that sent people into a frenzy. For years, the British public had been fobbed off that 'nothing could be done'. Now that someone was doing something – and succeeding – a different spirit was at work in the land.

England's football team breezed through the round of 32 in America. The opposition was weak, but it felt as if the squad were riding the same wave as the Buccaneers. President Pump understood television and was proud the tournament was in North America. He knew that football fans around the world were his kind of people.

It was too much to expect he wouldn't try to put himself at the centre of things. After a few games he began to truth his verdicts at the end of the match. With Gary Lineker and the BBC, this became a running joke. Post-match analysis would begin, then Gary would turn to the camera and announce that 'The verdict has now come in from a certain "local pundit".'

Pump knew he wasn't a football analyst, but he understood sports, crowds, and how to cut to the chase with his pithy eight-word summaries. His grasp of politics as part showbusiness was unrivalled since Bill Clinton. He also knew that if you dominated the public space, you left little room for your opponents. Gary clearly enjoyed his segues into what became known as 'Pump's Pearls.'

Gabriella kept up her four-a-week briefings, polished and confident, though she was keen to get the message out beyond Europe and America that the Channel was closed.

In Downing Street, the Prime Minister fumed at the mocking columns and *The Sun's* 'Politicians: Zero' scoreboard. But the Chancellor felt duty bound to point out that the Exchequer had already saved £2.5 billion on housing costs. The Home Secretary reported that asylum backlogs were shrinking, morale was up, and staff summer holidays were back on.

No one in government or anywhere else noticed the young man pacing Deal's streets at night. It was Pierre, Jean's son, scoping out the Vicarage, the Ribs and the harbour before slipping back across the Channel to report.

In July, Micah's two brothers arrived on leave from the Marines. Jake and Matt were delighted to meet Mr Bill, who sized them up in seconds with a naval eye. They longed to join a patrol but didn't want to intrude. Bill, knowing Philippe had asked for a few days off, decided they could cover him.

'Can Squint come too?' Jake teased.

'Don't call me that,' Micah snapped.

'But it is your name,' Matt pushed.

Micah's eyes flashed. 'Not here. They were fixed. Just drop it.'

Bill, sensing a row, stepped in. 'Let's just get some good footage on Thursday, shall we?'

The brothers grinned; Micah steadied himself. The Buccaneers had new allies on the water.

Chapter 24
The Hollywood Channel

The alarms rang early at the Vicarage and the hotel. Jake and Matt picked up Micah and drove him up the winding lanes to Margate.

'Other side of the road!' shouted Micah. The roads were empty, but he didn't want to die that morning.

Out on the water, Bill and the brothers were in their element. Jake and Matt listened carefully to the briefing and quickly fell in with the rest of the crew. They were on holiday, so no Buccaneer black uniforms – khaki with mirror shades was their choice.

All went smoothly until the engine in one Rib failed. Bill climbed aboard to fix it and handed Jake the radios.

'You're in charge now.'

'Affirmative. Yes, Sir,' Jake replied with Marine cadence.

For most of the morning, there was little to do except avoid large ships in the busy Channel.

'Let's try to get some decent footage, hey, Sq…Micah. What do you say?'

'That would be great. There are some shots we haven't got yet, if you're up for it?'

'If we're up for it?' Jake grinned. 'You bet we are.'

Micah explained his plan: a side-on shot of a Rib leaping from the wake of a large container ship, with France in the background. It was risky as he'd need to be in the water to get the best angle and because jumping a wake at 40 mph could flip the Rib.

'Well, there's no problem with the former,' Matt teased. 'We'll just toss you overboard!'

Having dropped Micah carefully into the sea, they ran a few practice jumps at slower speed to get the balance of the boat right. Then, when a tanker passed, they went for the full-speed leap. The Rib hit the wake beautifully – spray flying, the hull airborne for a heartbeat.

Then a horn blared from a freighter hidden behind the first tanker, a deep, dreadful sound that vibrated in the water. Jake and Matt saw it first, a wall of steel bearing down on their little brother.

'Can we make it?' shouted Jake.

'We have to!' yelled Matt.

Micah looked up at the vast ship looming above him, its shadow swallowing the light. With perfect timing, Jake lunged and grabbed him by the wrist, hauling him back aboard in one smooth pull.

'I didn't see it!' Micah gasped.

'Nor did I!' Matt admitted.

'And no one tells Mum!' Jake added firmly.

Exhilarated, they returned to the quayside, where Gabriella was waiting. She introduced them to Veronica Holmes from *History Today*, who was impressed by their easy Texan manners.

'Would you like to see your ancestral home on Monday?' Gabriella asked.

'And where would that be?' Jake replied.

Veronica checked her notes. 'Digging into your family tree, I discovered that one of your ancestors left Kent roughly two hundred years ago. He was the youngest child of a noble family and there's quite a tomb. I can show you on Monday and write an article about our visit, if you're happy with that?'

'We know a little of that story but none of the details. So, that would be a pleasure, Ma'am,' Jake said.

They arranged to meet at the Vicarage at 10 am, relieved after the day's early start to have a day off the water.

Later, Micah caught up with Gabriella for a debrief before heading to Deal to review the day's footage. He cut together a clip of his brothers' run, slowing the jump to a dramatic pause, and layered it with *The Boys Are Back in Town.* As Matt launched the Rib off the wake, Jake pivoted toward the camera, saluted in his mirror shades, and they slammed back down. The brief airtime beneath the boat made the stunt look like pure spectacle.

Micah uploaded the clip to Instagram. First, they'd shown British grit; then, French style. Now came a touch of American glamour. One of the first comments summed it up perfectly: 'Hollywood hits the Channel. Go USA!'

Across the street, unnoticed, a pair of scruffy men in caps watched the HQ, taking in every detail.

Chapter 25
While England Cheered

England were playing in the quarterfinals of the World Cup, which fell on a Friday night. The country was glued to their screens for the match against Uruguay. The roar of goals and crowds cheering echoed through living rooms, pubs and streets – oblivious to the drama about to unfold.

At 9 pm, a small boat crept toward Ramsgate. Pierre slipped into the water, swimming breaststroke toward the Ribs. With controlled fury, he sliced the first tank, then the next, on and on. All three Ribs deflated, just as his own boats had in France. Flush with revenge, he silently slipped back out of the harbour.

Meanwhile, his accomplice landed at the quayside, away from the Ribs. He crept into Harbour Street, poured lighter fluid through the letterbox of the HQ and tried to ignite it. The draught excluder blocked his first attempt, but eventually he managed to light a match, using the hinge as a shield. Flames caught the post and flyers on the floor and he retreated toward the harbour, rejoining his boat. Outside the wall, he picked up Pierre and even in the darkness, the two shared a grim smile.

To no one's surprise England's game had gone to a penalty shootout.

The pair motored across the bay toward the lights of the Deal pier. They pulled up just north of the Royal Hotel and waited silently on the beach, ready to melt into the darkness. Pierre's friend crept inland along Chapel Street, then cut down into St George's Passage. Barely ten feet wide, the ancient streets offered perfect cover. He crossed the High

Street and slipped into the churchyard between the building and the boundary wall. There he ignited the Molotov cocktail they had prepared and hurled it with a fierce throw at the Vicarage.

Inside, the Vicar, Kathryn, Micah and Gabriella were watching football. The roar of a scored penalty merged jarringly with the sudden shattering of glass, the whoosh of petrol igniting, and flames licking the front of the house.

'Quick! Everyone out the back door!' shouted the Vicar, grabbing his phone and urging them all to leave.

'Call the Fire Brigade! Are we all out? Whose got Tess?'

Kathryn called '999' and, with Gabriella, rushed round to the front to assess the damage. There was no sign of the Frenchman, who by now was back at the beach with Pierre.

'Micah, come with me. Let's grab the extinguishers from the church hall!'

Micah, young and nimble, dashed ahead. The Vicar followed, fumbling for his keys to unlock the hall. They grabbed two extinguishers and sprinted back to the house. Micah reached the flames first and began to fight the blaze, but the creeper on the front of the house was stubbornly crackling away. The Vicar arrived seconds later and handed Micah the second extinguisher.

'Here: try this from higher up; you're stronger than me.'

Standing on a garden table, Micah pressed the red button. A rush of white cloud smothered most of the flames. The fire brigade arrived moments later and doused the rest. Fortunately, the windows of the Vicarage had held, so the damage was almost entirely external.

Leslie quickly whatsapped supporters with a photo of the charred front door:

'We're okay. It's out. Are you all okay: please confirm.'

The football match roared on and England won the shootout after two glorious saves by their keeper. The nation cheered, unaware of the chaos in Deal.

Other Bucks sent messages confirming they were safe, but up in Ramsgate, the lads in the Royal Oak were just beginning to discover the local damage. Gabriella, shaken but composed, filmed a brief selfie video. Her hands trembled slightly, and though her sentences were calm and clear, her wide eyes betrayed her fear. Because she was normally so self-assured, seeing her shaken made the impact even greater.

She didn't know it yet, but England was about to become very protective. Many had tolerated the Buccaneers before – some with private sympathy, others with open admiration – but the attacks that night, especially the one on the Vicarage, changed everything. Gabriella had put herself out there for Britain and now that she was under attack, people wanted to defend her.

Micah's brothers arrived, fierce and protective.

'I'm fine. Really. I'm fine, Micah insisted, over and over.

The Buccaneers' boats were ruined. With great foresight, Bill had insisted the false front in the shop was made of fireproof material. It had cost extra, but it meant everything essential in the HQ was saved.

Early the next morning, Jean and his smugglers launched their biggest operation yet. It may have been cynical, but it was brutally effective. Wave after wave of boats set off and thousands of migrants began to land. No Buccaneer boats set out from Ramsgate that day; the Channel was wide open.

The newspapers only managed to print the football results the next morning, but online and on television the loop was relentless: the smouldering Vicarage and the clip of a shaken Gabriella. Jean and the other smugglers landed more than four thousand migrants that day, forcing the Home Office to cancel staff holidays to cope.

By midday it was all over and Jean had just thirty paid-up migrants left; one of whom was Abdul.

Bill sat on a folding chair outside the HQ and kicked himself silently. He hated the taste of failure. A night sentry was basic and obvious – he hadn't put one on. 'Never underestimate your enemy,' was a phrase that had saturated his career. Of all people, he should have known better.

News of the attacks spread everywhere. Photographs of the deflated Ribs and drone shots of the harbour were broadcast around the world. The provisional Home Office figures were stark and alarming. That morning, a tourist yacht had reported seeing at least eight bodies in the Channel's shipping lanes.

The Vicarage at Deal still smelled faintly of smoke. The two front windows were charred while the creeper looked doomed. The Vicar wanted to stay put and Kathryn wanted to clean, paint and put everything back in order. But they didn't think it was safe for Gabriella and Micah. They were all in shock, in different ways.

For a few tense hours, Gabriella and Micah slept at Alan and Leslie's. The house felt like a citadel, with its electric gates, cameras and high walls. Leslie moved them in with tea and blankets and that quiet, domestic competence that made people believe things would be all right. They tried to keep the pair's arrival hidden, for safety's sake.

The US Ambassador called, a gesture they appreciated and other messages from friends and strangers alike arrived at the HQ and the Vicarage. Deal and Ramsgate hummed with questions.

At noon, Gabriella announced she would hold the usual 5 pm press briefing. The Buccaneers hesitated, worried for her safety and the scrutiny it would invite. But she insisted she was fine – and that it was her duty. The press would be there, the public too. She wanted to say something that was true.

In the afternoon, she checked in with her prayer triplet. After sharing their concern and indignation, they prayed passionately for her. They hoped that somehow God would turn this assault on the Buccaneers into something positive. They all felt very far apart; it was the one moment on the trip when Gabriella longed for home. It was one thing to be abroad when things were going well but conflict, she realised, is always cultural.

By late afternoon, the north side of Ramsgate harbour began to fill. The press had to jostle the public for space in front of the Museum. Dave sensed the crowd would be bigger than usual and, in addition to the press feed, added a public address system so the public could hear. Micah, Alan and Gabriella met at the HQ working in the rooms untouched by fire. Four police officers came to escort them the few yards to the quay.

At 4.55 pm they stepped out onto the street, crossed the road and the first cheer went up. 'We love you, Gabby!' someone bawled in a broad Kent accent.

They walked along the Parade through a huge crowd, adorned in Buccaneer merchandise. It parted like the Red Sea for its new heroes. People had painted flags and messages on sheets and were waving them cheerfully: hearts, Stars and Stripes, Union Jacks and their names in black poster paint.

It wasn't necessary, but just as the press conference began, Randy Hooger appeared from the crowd. 'Ladies and gentlemen, we believe East Kent is one of the friendliest places in the world,' then he added with an impish grin, 'Is there a message we'd like to give to the Buccaneers to express our welcome?'

The harbour erupted with cheers. Cameras were live and running slightly late, but this was all anyone wanted to watch. With a steady step, Gabriella approached the microphone. Her hands were shaking but they steadied as she placed them on the lectern.

'Thank you,' she smiled. 'That means a lot to all of us.'

More cheers followed. At the back Micah's brothers watched proudly, sensing something bigger was unfolding.

'Last night,' Gabriella began, 'England won, but we lost. There were no Buccaneers today. As far as we know, more than four thousand migrants have landed illegally. Worse still, at least eight bodies have been found; people who didn't make it. St George's Deal will have to light more candles for those drowned overnight.'

She paused to let it settle. 'Two of the dead are women, five are men and one is a child.'

Her tone never broke, but the bluntness of her words stirred something: grief, anger and a sense of injustice.

'Bill says we've had the smugglers in a vice-grip,' she continued. 'Last night, they fought and took a breath.' She looked straight into the cameras: 'We need new boats. We will not give in.'

The crowd roared back, '*No!*'

'We will not give up.'

'No!'

'And we will put our foot straight back on their neck.'

That last sentence was later described as Churchillian. How had a young woman from the American Midwest rediscovered the fighting spirit once so common in England?

The crowd rumbled like thunder; approval, grief, the fierce energy of people unwilling to feel powerless. No one pressed for questions. Gabriella asked instead for a moment of quiet.

Micah stepped forward and read from Psalm 35, his voice trembling only at the edges:

'May those who seek our lives
be disgraced and put to shame;
may those who plot our ruin
be turned back in dismay.
May they be like chaff before the wind,
with the angel of the Lord driving them away;
may their path be dark and slippery,
with the angel of the Lord pursuing them.'

At the Amen, the crowd erupted again; not just applause but something like relief, as if faith had handed them a lifeline.

That night in Washington, President Ronald Pump had reached the end of his patience. He rang Sir Piers, brow furrowed, demanding action. 'These are American lives,' he said bluntly. His tweet was short, brash and effective: 'Go Buccaneers. The USA is right behind you!' Flag emojis of the United States, UK and France followed. It was a simple signal of solidarity that spread fast.

The English were embarrassed they hadn't protected their guests. The irony that they were there to protect England from uninvited guests only deepened the sense of shame. Sir Piers Starter made a statement that evening. The right words, perhaps, but the wrong tone.

Back in Deal, at midnight, Bill's phone buzzed. An old Navy friend, now in defence contracting, was on the line. 'Three boats are arriving for 3 am,' he said. 'Use them for as long as you need.'

'Top job,' Bill replied, the old sea grin returning for the first time in twenty-four hours.

True to his word in the early hours, three Pacific-24 Ribs slid calmly into the dock at Ramsgate. Bigger, faster, tougher than anything they'd used before. The handover agent demonstrated their controls in the low light, his hands moving with practised ease.

‘Press this for the python, the retractable spike. And careful, she bites. This one’s boost mode. Gentle, though, she can be very quick.’

The boats were larger than Bill would have preferred, but any boat was better than none. Each carried a flag on a short post beside the twin engines: a British ensign, neatly adapted with the Buccaneer logo stitched in the corner.

Bill smiled. Even the boats were ‘on brand’.

He stood at the quay and watched the men strap in, feeling that familiar surge; readiness and the clean nerves that come before action. He sent a short text to the wider group: ‘Three new boats have arrived. We’re back on.’

The Buccaneers were heading back to sea; their purpose sharpened by fire and adversity. The vice-grip on the Channel was returning.

Chapter 26
A Monumental Event

Veronica turned up at St George's as planned, at 10 am on Monday. In all the excitement, the Wildman brothers had nearly forgotten. But with five minutes to go, Micah suddenly remembered their history date, and they all rushed out to meet her.

Veronica was kind and unflappable. In the car, she gently asked Micah to retell the story of the previous Friday. It was strangely therapeutic for him; he hadn't slept well since and speaking it aloud helped. As they climbed the hill towards Chilham, the Texans wondered what they might find.

Veronica pulled up in the square and they all marvelled at the higgledy-piggledy Tudor architecture. Some houses had upper floors that protruded over the street. Wisteria and climbing roses completed the picture.

Unused to pubs, Jake hoped they might be visiting *The White Horse*. He couldn't believe the sign saying it was a '15th century establishment'. Matt, facing the other way, spotted the castle. But Veronica, seeing their looks, said, 'We'll have lunch at *The White Horse* later. The castle is closed. First things first. Let's go and see St Mary's.'

The church had flint walls and parapets, a typical parish church that had been extended and reworked over the centuries. The black octagonal clock face sat too high on the tower. Veronica wanted them to explore for themselves, so she simply invited them in through the ancient West door and said, 'Let's have a look around.'

St Mary's was full of natural light. A blue fleur de Lys carpet runner lined the central aisle. It was clearly a much-loved building and the brothers were awed by the age and beauty of the stone interior. They began studying the plaques on the wall, hunting for a Wildman.

The Lady Chapel had a monument with four people around a central pole. Interesting, but not theirs. They passed respectfully through the chancel and into a side chapel, where a sad scene in stone caught their eye: a young man, a child and a woman gathered around the central figure of a father, who they were mourning. The monument was slightly cramped by a piano and a stack of Gopak tables.

Matt saw it first. 'James Wildman,' he read aloud. They translated the Roman numerals. 'He died in 1816.'

'Oh my gosh, is he really a relative?'

Veronica nodded. 'Yes, I believe he's an ancestor of yours from about two hundred years ago.'

The brothers looked on with fascination. The display card said the sculpture was by a man called Chantrey, commissioned by James Wildman's widow and children. It also mentioned that he had been survived by three brothers.

The boys knew from family lore that their great-great-great-great-great-grandfather had left England for a better life in the New World, leaving three brothers behind. This must have been one of them, making him a distant uncle.

As Jake turned in profile, he looked remarkably like the profile on the memorial. Veronica was delighted; she had her story. She took several pictures of the three Wildman brothers in front of their ancestors. But more than that, she had ignited a passion for history in them, which pleased her most of all.

Micah had already grown fond of Kent, but knowing this was where his family had come from gave the county a new, deeper poignancy.

As might be expected, he decided to make a film about what he called this 'monumental' event. He persuaded Jake to pose in profile with their uncle's silhouette behind him. He sent the short film to his family and to Gabriella, just checking it was okay, before sharing it more widely. When it did go live, it added a gentle touch of humanity to the Buccaneer story.

The next day, Jake and Matt had to fly back to their station in Miami. Micah was sad to see them go as he had appreciated having his brothers around.

Chapter 27
Stalemate in Westminster

Across the Channel, the migrant camps looked emptier than they had in years. Fewer than a hundred men wandered about, listless and restless. Meanwhile, the Buccaneers continued patrolling, Bill and the team growing steadily more confident with their new, fearsome-looking boats.

In London, the political situation remained frozen. Sir Piers Starter didn't know which way to turn. Stopping the crossings was clearly good from a safety perspective and the savings in government spending were a godsend. But politically, he was exposed. The Buccaneers made the government look impotent.

That week, Randy Hooger raised a question during Prime Minister's Questions. After paying tribute to the courage of his constituents, he asked pointedly, 'Will the Royal Navy ever be deployed?'

It was a question many were now asking. How could increased defence spending be justified if the Navy couldn't be used to defend the realm? Within the service itself, frustration was spreading. Some admirals were tetchy at being shown up, while many ratings were desperate to join the fight. Watching ex-colleagues appear in glossy videos with thumping soundtracks was more than some could bear.

Sir Piers knew the legal position: Britain couldn't intervene militarily in French waters and mid-Channel interceptions were considered dangerous. Enough migrants had died already without risking more lives at the hands of the Royal Navy. He tried to make the best of being stuck, but it was increasingly unsatisfactory – a stalemate he could neither celebrate nor escape.

Chapter 28
The Invitation

Alan and Leslie were enjoying having Micah and Gabriella to stay. And to be honest, for the young pair, it was quite the upgrade. 'The Beach' was a fancy street and Gabriella's new bedroom had a balcony overlooking the sea – the perfect place for her morning coffee and prayers as the sun rose over the Channel.

One evening at dinner, the intercom buzzed.

'Oh, who's that?' said Leslie, a little frustrated.

Alan pressed the button. 'Hello?'

A broad Kentish accent replied. 'So sorry to disturb you all. It's Gary from The Stag. We just wondered if you'd like to join us to watch the World Cup tomorrow. It's quite something in The Stag when the football's on – and, well, we just thought the Yanks might enjoy it too.'

Alan knew Gary and The Stag well. He smiled at his guests. 'You're on speaker, my friend.'

Gary laughed. 'No need to book in. Just come along. Drinks will be on us. We all think the Bucks are terrific.'

Alan turned to the others. 'Ever been to a pub, gang?'

Micah and Gabriella exchanged embarrassed looks. They hadn't. Their campus was dry and in both their homes alcohol was frowned upon. Bars, where they came from, were viewed with suspicion – the haunts of alcoholics and troublemakers. Still, Gabriella had seen pubs on *Miss Marple* episodes and was quietly curious. She also knew that CS Lewis and JRR Tolkien, two of her heroes, had discussed their books in a pub.

Alan and Leslie had grown very fond of their guests. Alan admired Gabriella's mix of grace and steel, and he always appreciated competence. Micah, ever 'Mr Helpful,' had won Leslie over entirely. She hoped some of his good manners might rub off on Alan.

Leslie noticed their hesitation. 'They do serve non-alcoholic drinks, you know. And The Stag's just round the corner – you can always come home if you don't like it.'

Micah looked at Gabriella, then spoke for them both. 'This is a mighty kind invitation, and I think we'd like to say yes. But we're a dry school, so I think we need to check in with Naylor first before we can say for sure.'

Alan struggled to understand the idea of being barred from pubs, but he kept his counsel. Leslie smiled. 'Better to message him tonight, since the game is on tomorrow.'

Chapter 29
A Call from Sheila

At the Vicarage, the diocese had already sent round a team to repair the windows. The Vicar was grateful, though he noted – unkindly and only to himself – that the Bishop had never dropped by before. 'Perhaps I should have my house burnt down more often,' he pondered ruefully. He pushed the thought away and greeted Bishop Sheila with a smile.

For her part, the Bishop couldn't stand the Buccaneers. She tolerated their popularity as one might tolerate a child learning the recorder: unpleasant, but temporary. Secretly, she felt her authority threatened. The Vicar had become the most popular clergyman in England and had even been invited to present *Thought for the Day* on *Radio 4* – something she had coveted for years. That he could take it or leave it made her all the more cross.

'Well, how are you?' she asked brightly.

'It's all been a bit of a shock, to be honest.'

She nodded sympathetically. Sympathy was something she did well and, in this case, she even felt it.

'And how are you inhabiting your new public presence?' She nearly said 'notoriety' but corrected herself just in time.

'Well,' said the Vicar, 'to be honest, I feel the Buccaneers are an answer to prayer.'

Bishop Sheila recoiled but gestured graciously, 'Please, tell me more.'

'You'll remember,' he began, 'a couple of years ago I was walking the dog on the beach early one morning when a body washed up right in front of me. I pulled her out – Maryam Ali, from Somalia. She'd tried to cross the Channel, her boat sank and she drowned. Ever since then, we've lit a candle for every migrant who's died. That's one hundred and fifty so far. And I've been praying that God would bring an end to this suffering.'

The Bishop bristled. She disliked anyone implying that God might answer the prayers of the country's closet racists, as she saw them. Still, she kept her composure and managed a polite, 'How fascinating.'

'Yes,' said the Vicar, 'It's been amazing to see how God brought together just the right people at just the right time.'

That was too much for the bishop. 'And what of authority?' she snapped primly. 'Isn't this a matter for those in power? We can't all go around doing whatever we want.' Her view was simple: the government ruled, the church supported and guided. The Buccaneers were turning this on its head with their so-called initiative. She looked forward to her seat in the House of Lords, imagining people hanging from her every word.

The Vicar wasn't finished. 'Well, we'd all be delighted if the government would actually govern, that's the ideal. But this has been going on for years. People are drowning, often in the dark and cold. It's simply not right.'

He sensed he'd gone far enough and added gently, 'I do agree though, that the Buccaneers are the second-best option, for sure.'

Bishop Sheila liked that he'd acknowledged the proper order of things. They prayed together and she left soon after.

At lunchtime, he was still fuming. Poor Kathryn received the full download.

'The Establishment is a just a solution-free zone,' his frustration in full flow, 'They're just patronising twits who won't lift a finger to help.'

The Vicar had always been a 'local church' man, never much interested in committees or climbing the ecclesiastical ladder. Kathryn looked on and thought this was probably for the best.

Chapter 30
The Stag and The Statesman

President David FaceTimed Gabriella and Micah the next morning. He was proud of them; they were raising Naylor's profile around the world. Once he was satisfied they were safe in their new home they then asked about pubs. He laughed and confessed that he'd once been to one himself while at Cambridge. He gave them permission to go, so long as no alcohol was consumed.

Both were delighted and thought they'd better ask their prayer triplets to pray for 'protection.' But their friends saw through this and knew they were just 'flexing' their upcoming pub trip. They wished them well, nonetheless.

The Stag is a handsome, three-bay public house on the seafront in South Deal. As they approached, the ship's wheel above the door gleamed in the evening light. When the four of them walked in, Gary spotted them from behind the horseshoe bar and smiled broadly. The soft glow of filament bulbs adding to the sense of welcome.

'You're here! Drinks are on us. What'll it be?'

Leslie ordered a gin and tonic, Alan a pint of Old Speckled Hen. Micah, having done a bit of online research, asked for a pint of Lucky Saint, and Gabriella decided to play it safe with a Coke.

Three TVs glowed in various parts of the pub, with people standing and sitting all around. Anticipating their arrival, Gary had saved them the best table, perfectly positioned in the window, so no one blocked their view of the screen.

England were playing Brazil. Despite a strong run, national expectations could best be described as 'cautiously optimistic.' Before kick-off, fans unfurled a huge banner – at least twenty-five yards across. Usually, it bore only the red cross of St George, but this time something was different. A large red heart appeared in the centre and across the top, the word *England.*

'Well, England loves something,' said Gary Lineker. 'Let's see what.'

Micah and Gabriella leaned forward, sensing something was afoot. As the banner unfurled fully, the words 'The Buccaneers' appeared underneath.

'Oh, that's a nice touch,' Lineker added. 'It's been a tough week for the Bucks back home.'

No one in The Stag heard him. The moment the words appeared, the pub erupted. Cheers, whistles, glasses raised. Leslie even shed a quiet tear, though no one noticed amid the pats on the back and good-natured hugs.

After ninety minutes, the score was still 0-0. Both sides played superbly, the tension electric. President Pump had already retruthed a photo of the England Flag offering his support to the Bucks. Now he felt it was time to comment on the football: 'Soccer's great, but these games need more goals!' The BBC team chuckled, one pundit quipping, 'Sherlock Holmes's job isn't in danger tonight.'

Though a few regulars had overindulged, Micah and Gabriella were having a marvellous evening. Neither of their hometowns had anything like a pub. The Stag wasn't seedy like a bar, had more atmosphere than a café and offered the easy sociability of standing conversation. People wandered over during the match to shake their hands.

'Great job, you guys!' was the refrain of the night. A few older men tried their luck asking Gabriella out, but Alan fended them off protectively.

Leslie's nerves could not stand a penalty shoot-out, so she was immensely relieved when Kane scored in the 105th minute. The pub went wild. Fifteen agonising minutes later, despite Brazil's desperate efforts, the final whistle blew.

Pump truthed again: 'See, it's much better with goals!' For once, support was transatlantic.

Behind the scenes, however, the President was already thinking several moves ahead. With his advisers he had worked out that Britain and France could, in theory, adjust their maritime borders to create a joint security zone in the Channel. This would enable the Royal Navy to act at the French coast, and vice versa.

At the moment, Sir Piers was refusing to send the Royal Navy into French waters to stop the boats from setting off. President Macaroon could never allow it either. But if the Channel were reclassified as a joint security zone stretching eighty miles from north to south, everyone could save face – and the Navy could take over.

The Channel is one of those odd places in the world where geography and legal realities collide. A country's territorial waters extend twelve miles from its shoreline. But with the waterway only twenty-one miles across, there is a three-mile overlap in the middle. This 'confusion' provided the legal flexibility to reclassify the entire Channel.

Pump's advisers had sounded out both governments discreetly. There were no legal obstacles – especially if the agreement expired after a set period – only a lack of political will. The President was patient. He lingered at the center of his web, confident the moment to act would come, as it always did.

Chapter 31
Abdul's Resurrection

Bill was still keen to keep his vice-grip on the smugglers, but by mid-July there was no escaping the fact that attempts to cross were down. The message must be getting through. Gabriella's updates were almost becoming routine, except for Ryan Davis at *The Times*. His penetrating questions were sharper than most and the way he smiled at Gabriella had nearly knocked her off guard a couple of times.

In the football, England romped to a 4–0 win against Croatia, and the country shook off some invisible shackle as it celebrated wildly. After the USA had been knocked out, President Pump had thrown himself fully behind the England team, threatening tariffs on their opponents. Apparently, it was only a joke, but with Pump you were never sure. At the end of the tournament, he truthed in full caps: 'THE BEST WORLD CUP THERE HAS EVER BEEN', a message no one in England would argue with.

The England crowd at the final had managed to disgrace itself by chanting obscene songs about their own Prime Minister, then following it up with chants of, 'Pump, Pump, We love you!' After one of the goals, England players imitated Pump's signature dance. The President beamed from ear to ear; he knew a win when he saw one.

After the final on Sunday, whoever was going to take the Monday morning slot would be pulling the short straw. Philippe was back from his break, and Alan and Leslie felt they should take one for the team. 'But 3.30 am, after winning the World Cup? Really?'

As the Joneses rushed over the Channel, they had been allocated the Southern sector, beyond Cap Gris Nez. It was always hard to predict what the smugglers would try and today they were intent on a major launch from Audresselles.

Jean had retired after his World Cup semi-final triumph; or at least that's how he saw it. So far, no one had worked out who had petrol-bombed the Vicarage. There were no witnesses and the youngsters had carefully avoided CCTV. Some grainy doorbell footage existed, but in the dark, the smugglers felt reasonably safe.

Pierre, Jean's son, still had four large boats to use that he had ordered in happier times. Abdul was surprised to receive a text from him but took it in good faith and made his way south from Calais to the dunes to be ready for the morning. He texted his family and sent numerous messages to friends. He kept with him a small plastic bag for his phone and passport. The smugglers had suggested arriving with nothing, but Abdul knew his brother was coming to Kent to meet him. They hadn't seen each other for eleven years and both were genuinely excited about the reunion.

Since the Bucks had grown in popularity, and with the weather improving, there was no shortage of 'birdwatching' recruits. There were so many offers that they had to cut it down to two-day shifts. Today's couple were sharp; they saw the boat fall out of the van and sent a pin immediately. Puncture drones were dispatched, but Abdul and the migrants had their tennis rackets ready and volleyed them away with ease.

Bill picked up the 'albatross' message and roared around the point, Philippe readying himself for action. But the new smuggling team was quicker – they were already at the shoreline, merely seconds from heading out to sea.

'Hold on!' he shouted at Philippe as he pushed the boost button, for something extra. Alan, watching from his boat, thought they might have hit eighty miles per hour. The noise was tremendous. Pierre had even given some of his migrants long spikes, as if they were to be harpooning whales from the front of the boat.

It was over in a heartbeat. Philippe jumped into the sea with the boat still at dangerous speeds, but he used the momentum to launch his swim. He was under the inflatable in twenty seconds, narrowly avoiding the spikes and the outboard. How many stabs had the boat received? He wasn't sure and minutes later waited helplessly offshore to be picked up. As he made his turn Bill was preparing the python just in case.

***

As the inflatable drifted out to sea it deflated, but too slowly. One by one, the migrants dropped into the water. Later it was revealed there were thirty-six on board. Sixteen were strong swimmers and made it back to shore. Fourteen had life jackets and though swept out to sea, were easily picked up by Alan and Leslie. But six, including Abdul, had no life jackets and were caught in a riptide.

Abdul was terrified by the black boat bearing down on them. Had he seen someone fall out? Then he saw a black sliver in the water, and before he knew it, the boat was deflating. Pandemonium ensued. In multiple languages, people asked what to do.

'Shore or boat?' Abdul screamed as he slid into the sea, his clothes weighing him down as the water saturated them.

It was very much every person for themselves. Abdul decided to head for an expensive-looking yacht just offshore. Perhaps it would take him to England? Alan and Leslie realised the danger everyone was in and headed slowly towards the shore and the throng of splashing bodies. They thought they had counted thirty-six through the binoculars and this was confirmed by the first arrivals, who clambered up at the back. Part of the ruse was that they weren't a coordinated team, so they feigned surprise at this 'awful accident'.

Two people were still missing. Leslie saw one drifting frozen in fear past *The Girl Kathleen*. The crew shouted at him and managed to awaken him enough that he stretched out an arm and was pulled to safety. Normally, the swim deck at the back was used to bathe in warmer climes. Today, it was being used as a vital part of a rescue operation. As they chugged slowly on, Alan saw a last person, face down in the sea. The body seemed to hug the boat as they moved gently forward. Alan and a crew member leant out and caught it, swinging the body up onto the swim deck. They rolled it over and Alan looked down at him and noticed his kind face.

'Give him mouth-to-mouth, Alan!' shouted Leslie from the top deck.

'Mouth-to-mouth? He's dead!'

'He might not be; give it a try!' She was busy helping other migrants into dry clothes, ironically Buccaneer tracksuits.

Alan hesitated.

'Look, if you don't do it, I'll come down there and give him mouth-to-mouth myself.'

The prospect of his wife performing CPR on a dead male migrant galvanised Alan. Bill had trained the team before the season began and it kicked in. Hold the nose, blow, push the chest, repeat. Even though Abdul had Afghan colouring, his face was blue. Leslie looked up to heaven and prayed: 'Please Lord, don't let this man die today.'

Almost immediately Abdul sputtered, coughed up water and took a huge gasping breath. Then another. And another.

He looked at Alan and asked in Farsi, 'Am I in hell?'

'Me, Alan,' said his rescuer with hand gestures.

As Abdul's blood filled with fresh oxygen his memory began to return. He recalled the weight of his wet clothes pulling him under and as that happened, he remembered looking up at the face of the kind looking woman on the yacht, then darkness.

As he continued to breathe his hearing returned and he slowly realised the man next to him was speaking English.

'Me, Alan.'

'I am Abdul,' he replied in perfect English.

'Welcome aboard!'

After tea and biscuits, Abdul began to revive, even managing to stand. It was an hour and a half round to Calais and Leslie didn't want him to get cold. She persuaded him to change into clean clothes in the cabin. Abdul carefully stowed his passport and phone in his new clothes.

'Where shall I put the old ones, please?' he asked politely.

Leslie pointed to black bin liners, offering him a choice to keep them or discard them.

The Patrollers rarely had to pick up migrants, since the aim was for them to make it back to shore before interception. This time, with twenty migrants aboard, the situation was delicate. Alan, Leslie, and the crew were outnumbered and keen to avoid any hint of mutiny. More tea and biscuits were offered, but as they passed Cap Gris Nez, it became clear they were heading for the port of Calais – not England.

'We have paid good money to go to England!' protested Abdul loudly.

'Unfortunately, not with us,' replied Alan tactfully. 'We are going for lunch in Calais and that's as far as we can take you. We'll drop you off there.'

Abdul was unhappy. 'There is no money in Afghanistan. I cannot go back there. My brother is in England. I want to go and work with him.'

'There must be some money in Afghanistan,' said Alan. 'People aren't starving there.'

'That's true, but our family business needs money, and the Taliban have closed the banks.'

'What business is that?' said Alan, genuinely interested.

'We have a family pharmacy in Lashkargah.'

‘So, you’re a pharmacist?’ said Alan doubtfully. ‘Well, I’m a pharmacist too.’

Neither believed the other. They quizzed each other, Alan asking professional questions, Abdul responding in kind. Even though he had been unconscious a few minutes earlier there was nothing wrong with Abdul’s mind now and he gave as good as he got.

‘Boys, boys!’ said Leslie. ‘Calm down. It is possible you both might be pharmacists.’

They sat quietly for a few minutes, brooding. Leslie wondered who would speak first.

Eventually, Alan asked, ‘So, this alleged pharmacy; where is it and what it’s like?’

Abdul explained and showed him on Google Maps. It seemed a good location with good footfall. Abdul explained that the banking and credit system had collapsed; he could sell drugs easily but lacked the capital to pay the new extortionate rates for stock, sanctions were biting hard. He was going to England to save the family business.

‘How will you get funds back home?’

‘Via bitcoin first, then dollars in the future.’

Alan had invested in two hundred pharmacies over the years, with only six failures. He recognised talent and character, and if Abdul had wanted to open a pharmacy in Haselmere, he would have backed him. Now he was weighing whether to support Abdul in his own country, though investing in Afghanistan seemed far riskier.

He wanted to ask Leslie’s opinion, but it was too public a place. He didn’t like being rushed, but the port was approaching. As he paused for mental clarity, he felt a strange tide lifting him higher to a better vantage point. Leslie had been listening to them chat and somehow she sensed what Alan wanted to know. She winked at him, before adding diplomatically: ‘Afghanistan is a place I’ve always wanted to visit.’

'Right,' said Alan, looking squarely at Abdul. 'We don't have that much time but I want to propose a deal. I'm offering to give you cash for a flight home. Once things clear up here, we'll come to Afghanistan, and I want to see if I can invest in your pharmacy. That's my business and I can tell even now that you are good at it.'

Abdul hesitated. He was in a terrible situation. He wanted desperately to see his brother – but his boat had been sabotaged, and he had nearly drowned. He was about to disembark in France, where he would be stranded, jobless, and running out of funds. His earlier confidence had faded, and now there was this couple offering help. He paused, weighing his options.

'Okay. I will accept your deal. Allahu Akbar.'

He stood up and offered Alan his hand to shake. His comment about Allah caught Alan off guard and in a nervous moment he told Abdul, 'Best to speak to the missus about God. She's the believer.'

'You aren't a believer?' asked Abdul.

'No,' said Alan. 'All that God stuff is not for me.'

For Abdul, this tipped the scales in his mind back the other way.

'I'm afraid the deal's off. Honestly, I can't go into business with an infidel.'

Alan bristled at the word 'infidel' and he stood up for a second row. With fingers pointing and voices raised Abdul pressed Alan on why he didn't believe. In the heat of the moment he blurted out the truth, something he had tried for a long time to stow below the surface.

'My wife and I struggled to have children, which we prayed about a lot. As she lay on the bed crying after her last miscarriage – her fifth – I decided there and then I was done with God.'

Abdul paused. Then he sat down to lower the temperature. Alan and Leslie looked at each other; a plaster had been ripped off. While she knew he had found their inability to have children difficult, up until that moment she didn't quite realise the extent of his anger and pain.

Abdul shared, in Farsi, while gesturing at Alan: 'Iman kabud shodeh' – a 'bruised believer.' Alan could see himself in that phrase and for a moment they were quiet again.

The boat was now entering Calais' huge harbour. Having both sized each other up, with surprising calm, they shook hands on a deal. Alan popped into the cabin and discreetly gave Abdul €1,000 to hide in his shoes just as the French police arrived to escort the migrants away.

After lunch, it was a little flat on the journey back to Ramsgate, but Alan and Leslie felt that they had been jolted forward by a hidden force.

Later, in the bar, the story became legend. Dave joked, coughing and spluttering, 'Can I have 1,000 euros too?!' Bill joined in offering his shoe as a hiding place. Then Colin started puckering up and with a terrible Afghan accent asked, 'Can I get some mouth-to-mouth please?' They called the day his 'French bromance with Abdul.' Alan wasn't going to be allowed to forget this quickly.

When he arrived home, he told Leslie how much they had all laughed. She agreed she'd never seen him act so rashly, but as she kissed him goodnight she added, 'In for a penny, in for a pound. Afghanistan, here we come!'

Chapter 32
A Change in the Air

As the summer wore on, the England team returned in triumph from the USA. Vast crowds greeted the parades in London and Manchester.

Ryan Davis was nothing if not persistent, and as July progressed, he began lingering after press conferences, hoping for a chance to invite Gabriella for a drink. She was charm personified and managed to evade his interest with effortless poise, though inwardly she longed for an hour with him to discuss their PR operation from the other side. She knew, however, there was no such thing as a purely social relationship with a journalist.

Ryan found her beguiling. He could not quite fathom her or the source of her talents. If only he could spend a little time with her, when she would let her guard down, he believed he might solve these mysteries.

The Vicar was beginning to encourage Micah and Gabriella to think about their departure on August 11th. They had visited nine schools and had become regulars at St George's in Deal. At first, they had been taken aback by the expectations of a Church of England primary school. The headteacher, Helen Bones, had prayed with them before asking them to read Bible stories, sing and lead the children in prayer.

After the firebombing of the Vicarage, some pupils had come to the front in an assembly to lay hands on them and offer sweet prayers of protection. In American schools, all this would have been banned – at first their heads spun – but over time it offered a real-world lesson in a different model, with all its strengths and quirks.

Once, as they were leaving the school, a little girl called Tilly ran over clutching a card. 'Look! It's an angel protecting you and Micah!' The drawing was unclear, but Micah and Gabriella treasured Tilly's thoughtfulness.

One evening at the bar, Dave reported that Primark had paid over their licensing fee for May, and the Buccaneers were now £300,000 richer. Bill joked it might last the night, but thinking of the students' imminent departure, the team began to consider hiring professional PR help.

As usual, Gabriella was ahead of the curve. She decided to use Ryan Davis's interest to her advantage. Much to his surprise, she now agreed to a drink – but at the bar, she pressed him for the best PR firms in London. He obligingly provided names, though when he realised her interest was prompted by her departure, he looked at her a little forlornly. He had been trying to write a profile of her, but it felt incomplete. He was dogged in his pursuit of the truth.

Then, in a moment of inspiration, he asked casually if she had 'made it to France yet.' Normally, she would have dashed through the Channel tunnel like a shot, but as the public face of the Buccaneers she had been hesitant.

'Look,' Ryan said, 'How about Friday – your day off – I pick you up and take you to Boulogne? We could have moules frites and see some of these famous beaches.'

Gabriella paused. She did want to see France, but she had no intention of starting a romantic relationship with Ryan. Yet her reply was subtler than either expected.

'I'd love to come but just to be clear and I hope I'm not presuming, this is purely a work trip. Naylor doesn't allow romantic relationships while we're on our missions.'

She could have said she didn't want a romance, but by framing it as a Naylor's rule, she removed the personal aspect, something they both noticed.

'Of course,' Ryan said. 'France on Friday – a romance free zone!'

They both laughed.

Chapter 33
Talking Texan with the WI

Before he left, Micah had to fulfil his obligation to speak at a joint meeting of the East Kent WI. The Vicar had warned him that at his training college, as well as being trained in Pauline theology, they had been drilled never to cross the flower ladies, or the Women's Institute. This was certainly a talk to prepare for and, as he put it, 'polish your shoes.'

For their summer spectacular, two hundred ladies gathered with Micah at Walmer Castle. The committee sat in a row at the top table, with Micah beside the chairwoman, Lady Eliza Barrington. She had no trouble being called 'Ma'am' and seemed to warm to the Texan, even though he was young enough to be one of her grandchildren.

After singing *Jerusalem*, Lady Eliza rose to thank the Warden of the Cinque Ports for their hospitality and to thank the ladies for attending. She was a formidable woman and not afraid to show it. She introduced Micah with warm applause and he rose to speak.

Why Micah had agreed to talk on 'The flora and fauna of Texas' he had no idea, but he gave it his best shot. He began with the bluebonnet and the devil's pincushion, moved on to longhorn cattle, and finished with armadillos, lizards and alligators. Mercifully, the five minutes flew by, and relieved, he asked for questions.

'Do you have any poisonous snakes?' asked a rich, plummy voice.

Micah hadn't thought to mention snakes, assuming they were everywhere. 'Well, which ones do you have here, Ma'am? And I'll tell you if we have any extras.'

The same voice replied: 'We only have the boring old adder and its bite is like a bee sting. I thought yours might be a little wilder.'

Micah could hardly believe England had no lethal snakes. As he sped through rattlers, copperheads and the super-deadly coral snake, the audience warmed to him. Questions flowed and he was clearly good on his feet.

After a few minutes, Lady Eliza stood, fixed Micah with a look and asked if he was prepared to take questions about the Buccaneers. He was surprised there had been none so far, but when he nodded, Lady Eliza addressed the audience.

'Ladies, our guest is prepared to take questions on this most controversial summer.' Despite her attempts to avoid the topic about fifty hands shot up. They had clearly been waiting for permission to stray from Texan flora and fauna.

'Did you know about the Buccaneers before you came?'

'No, Ma'am.'

'Do you think the Prime Minister should send in the Royal Navy?'

'Well, this isn't my country, Ma'am, so I couldn't say. But you're asking a sensible question.'

He was diplomatic, clear and charming. At the end, the final question was:

'What has been the highlight of your trip?'

'Visiting St Mary's, Chilham and seeing the statue by Sir Francis Chantrey, in honour of my great-great-great-great uncle, James Wildman. Without a doubt, Ma'am, that was the greatest privilege for me and my brothers.' Unbeknown to Micah making a historical reference that bonded the two countries together, while expressing love for one of their churches – he had hit the jackpot.

Lady Eliza concluded by thanking him for the talk and when he offered to pray for the WI, they could hardly refuse. As they clapped at the end, Micah noticed a few ladies discreetly wiping away tears.

Word got back to the Vicar the next day when Lady Eliza rang with her report: 'He is a very fine young man; he made Texas proud.' It wasn't effusive, but the Vicar knew that with Lady Eliza that was as good as it gets. And when you have the WI on your side, you are unstoppable.

Chapter 34
The Philosophy of Philippe

Abdul had made it safely home and texted Leslie to say so. Apparently, the airfare had only been five hundred euros, though he'd needed to offer some 'encouragement' to the border guard to let him back into his own country. His family were delighted at his return – worried about their prospects, yes, but thrilled by his tale of near-death and miraculous rescue by 'Mr Alan'.

The August edition of *Vanity Fair* dropped in the United States in late July. On the cover was a photo of Philippe, dressed immaculately in a tailored navy suit. The feature essay was titled 'The Philosophy of Philippe: What Drives the Channel Buccaneer.' It was surprisingly thoughtful; Philippe did a fine line in Proust, Rousseau and Jean-Paul Sartre. Yet readers seemed at least as interested in the accompanying photo spread: Philippe on a Hawaiian beach, emerging from the surf, diving under a waterfall, and reclining, rather artfully, in an assortment of French swimming trunks. Sales in the U.S. were tremendous. It turned out that people wanted Philippe on their coffee table, not just on their screen.

President Pump noticed some of his staff flicking through *Vanity Fair* in the West Wing.

'Just reading up on your French philosophy?' he quipped to Carolyn, his Press Secretary.

'Yes, sir,' she replied. 'I'm all over that... philosophy.'

That morning, Pump was meeting with the Navy chiefs to discuss U.S. fleet deployments around the world. He signed off on the usual rotations, approving the Dwight D Eisenhower strike group to return across the Atlantic after their time in the Mediterranean.

Back in Deal, Gabriella and Micah had only a few tasks left to complete. There was the farewell dinner in the church hall on Thursday, their final service on Sunday and then the trip to Gatwick airport on Monday. The PR handover had gone smoothly.

Ryan and Gabriella, meanwhile, had agreed to postpone their trip to France to her last Friday as the weather had been too awful for moules frites by the sea.

Chapter 35
Goodbyes to England

The farewell dinner on Thursday was surprisingly good. The Vicar, eager to fill the hall, had invited the Buccaneers, and Alan had generously 'upgraded' the food and wine. The result was a lively celebration with laughter, stories and a few hymns sung off-key. Alan did the Buccaneers proud with his warm thanks to Gabriella and Micah.

On Friday, Ryan beeped his horn outside Alan and Leslie's promptly at eight o'clock. Gabriella emerged in a pale blue summer dress, a fawn cardigan on her arm, sunglasses perched in her hair; a touch of American poise against the Kentish sky.

He whisked her off to the tunnel and, with the time change, they were in Boulogne by half past eleven. Over steaming bowls of moules frites, they peppered each other with questions. Ryan longed to get beneath her skin; he wanted to discover what truly made her tick.

Gabriella spoke of a walk she had had with the Vicar. 'He said people get excited about new gifts from God – healing, prophecy and so on. But sometimes, he said, pressure simply reveals the gifts you already have. I think that's what's happened to me.'

She told him of her childhood as the middle child of five. 'My younger brothers acted up for attention. My older sisters had age on their side. I always felt I had one shot to be heard, so I had to make it count.' She smiled. 'My mum's Canadian, too. I suppose that helped. Midwesterners are polite, but Canadians take it to a whole new level.'

Ryan listened, utterly fascinated. In these candid reflections, she revealed more of herself than in any other interview he had ever encountered, her honesty striking and unguarded.

After lunch – messy, delicious and far too large – they drove north along the coast, stopping at Cap Gris-Nez. The air was bright and clear, and from the lighthouse Gabriella saw the white cliffs of Dover for the first time. She gasped, surprised by the emotional tug. Ryan broke out into Vera Lynn's famous song about the white cliffs, but after a few bars thought better of it.

This stretch of water had been her world for weeks – the scene of danger, courage and triumph – but seeing it from France stirred her. She felt protective of the Channel; it had been her waterway to defend. She felt a pang of guilt too, thinking of the migrants who had stood on that same shore, dreaming of coming to England, while she had helped turn them away.

Ryan spread a rug in a sheltered spot and handed her a cornet of chouchou he'd bought at the market. 'A taste of France,' he said with mock solemnity. She laughed, nearly spilling them.

They lay back for a while, content in the sea breeze. Then Ryan asked, 'Can I take a picture of you? I need one for the article I'm writing about an American enigma.'

Gabriella hesitated, then smiled. 'Sure.'

He lifted his phone and clicked a couple of times. She was relaxed, her face sunlit, with the cliffs of Dover pale behind her. It was only a second, but it was a moment of intimacy.

On the ferry home, they leaned against the railings, the sea wind in their hair. Ryan talked of his childhood in North London: his mother, who corrected every lapse in grammar at the dinner table, and his father, who could never resist stopping to ask strangers how things worked. 'If I love words and I'm curious,' he said, 'it's definitely their fault.'

She enjoyed that he was interested in her as a person and not just as a spokesperson. At work he asked far more searching questions than any other journalist, but it came from genuine curiosity, and she liked that.

As they watched the coast draw nearer, there was a lull in the conversation – one of those moments that could go either way. Gabriella thought, fleetingly, that he might kiss her. But almost as soon as she had the thought the klaxon sounded and the captain asked them to return to the car deck. The moment passed.

At the house gate, they said their goodbyes.

'That's the best non-date I've ever been on,' she said.

He smiled. 'Friends?'

'For sure,' she replied and turned back inside.

On Sunday at church there were prayers, hugs and expressions of gratitude; by Monday morning, the end had come all too soon. Their flight was booked, their bags packed. Leslie drove them to the station to catch the 9.28.

As they pulled in, a surprise awaited. Word had spread and a sea of children from St George's filled Platform 1, waving Union Jacks and Stars and Stripes.

Led by Mrs Bones, they began to sing a modern version of *The Lord's My Shepherd*. Their small voices reached bravely for the descant, and as the sound filled the station, Gabriella leaned against Micah, tears streaming down her cheeks. She had not expected this – she had not expected to fall in love with Deal, hook, line and sinker.

And then, as if on cue, little Tilly appeared again, clutching another handmade card. 'The angel's flying with you to America!' she beamed. Gabriella knelt, hugged her tightly and tucked the picture safely into her bag.

Three cheers rang out as the train drew in with a rush. Gabriella and Micah waved from the windows as it pulled away, the children still singing and waving as the train slipped from view.

Chapter 36
The Costs and Colours of Duty

The Channel disaster came without warning.

It was supposed to be a routine patrol. Bill and Philippe had been catching up after what had clearly been a very lucrative trip to Hawaii. They had been alerted to a small inflatable pushing out from the shore side of the Calais channel, the route that took ferries speedily out to the open sea. Bill angled his Rib neatly through the rolling wash of the bigger ships and saw the inflatable ahead. People were boarding at the stern, but the bow looked empty, with no figures or movement, so Bill decided to deploy the python.

The heavy spike was lowered at the Rib's bow; its design enabling inflatable punctures with one thrust. Bill aimed cleanly, but the wake of a ferry lifted his boat from behind making the python drive harder and deeper than intended.

What Bill could not see, what no one could see, was the woman huddled in the prow. Small and hidden under a sheet of plastic, she had been invisible from beyond the boat. The python pierced the rubber and her body in the same moment. She was killed instantly.

Bill registered nothing, only the satisfying hiss of collapsing tubes. But Philippe, glancing sideways, caught the look of horror on the migrants' faces. For a split second, he thought he saw blood streaked on the metal before the sea washed it clean.

As is the modern way, it was all caught on film. A tourist on a passing ferry had been recording the Buccaneer cat and mouse. By the time they returned to harbour, the footage was already online.

The woman's name was Duwana Abdo. She was twenty-three years old, originally from Sudan. By evening, an earlier photograph of her in Calais – young, pretty and exhausted – was everywhere.

The Buccaneers convened at HQ. Bill, trained for a crisis, was calm, even apologetic. Gabriella had already flown home to the States, but she'd left 'talking points' in case of an accident. Their line was simple: One death is too many; operations are suspended.

At 5 pm, they made the announcement.

In Westminster, Sir Piers Starter saw his moment and he pounced. The Prime Minister appeared grim on camera, naming Duwana, praising her 'courage,' and declaring that 'this vigilante behaviour must stop.' He assured people that the government was in charge. It was a masterclass in empathy, or so his team thought.

But the Vicar made a subtler point. On the church's Instagram he lit a candle for Duwana, adding it to a table already ablaze with one hundred and fifty others; one for each migrant drowned. The message was unspoken but pointed: the Buccaneers had killed one, but the sea and the smugglers had killed many more. Gabriella saw the post and liked it from America.

A life had been taken and the world was watching. Bill knew that silence would be misread. If he was to answer for what had happened, he would do so on his own terms.

The press was merciless the next day. France announced an investigation and quickly made a formal request for Bill's arrest and extradition. Starter looked almost gleeful as he briefed the lobby on the UK's full cooperation with 'our European partners.' He was patronising, brought only slightly down to earth by the revelation later in the day that the Bucks had, so far, saved the taxpayer £5.5 billion.

Bill was tipped off that police would come at dawn. He didn't run. Instead, he prepared. He pressed his tropical white uniform, polished his shoes and carefully arranged every ribbon he had ever earned. Retirement gave him the freedom to wear them all: British, American, NATO and others that had never been spoken of.

At 3.30 am he rose, exercised, shaved and showered. By 5 am, two camera crews were in place. Sky News had rushed down first, tipped off by the Buccaneers' new PR team. They set up their tripods directly across from Bill's house. But they weren't alone. The BBC was already there, crouched in a hedge, cables snaking towards a silent camera. The government had given them the nod.

The rivalry was absurd: elbows jabbed, tripods clattered, microphones collided in the half-light. One cameraman nearly filmed the other rather than the house. Both crews muttered curses but kept their lenses trained. They could sense something big was about to unfold.

At 5.36 am, the police arrived, dressed as if this were a drug raid: black uniforms, visors down and 'The Enforcer' ram ready to smash down the door.

Bill saw them and flicked on his garden floodlights. Officers blinked as he stepped out of his front door, cap under his arm, ribbons gleaming in the dawn light.

'I will come willingly,' he said, steady as ever, 'if you let me raise my colours first.'

The cameras jolted awake. Sky shoved the BBC; the BBC shoved back. But both caught the moment: Bill advancing to the flagpole, the Union Jack climbing the rope, it snapping in the morning breeze, all set against the dawn glow. He saluted, placed his cap on and turned back to the officer in charge.

'Warrant Officer Bill Smith, reporting for duty.'

The pictures were dazzling, heroic and defiant; it would have been impossible to script.

When he saw the footage in the States, Micah knew exactly what to do. Within two hours he had cut the video to the tune of *Up Where We Belong* from *An Officer and a*

Gentleman. The Union Jack unfurled in time with the crescendo. Bill saluted as the music soared.

By the evening, his clip was everywhere. The hashtag #WayToGoPaula was trending, a cheeky nod to the film's heroine. Later on #FreeBill took over.

Starter pressed on that, 'Smith is a suspect in the brutal killing of Duwana Abdo and that this vigilantism must stop.' But the words jarred with the pictures. In his uniform Bill looked like duty personified, while Starter looked like he was handing out a parking ticket.

At lunchtime, the nation offered its view. On Radio 2, Jerry Klein fielded furious callers. One demanded a poll on X: 'Who would you arrest? Bill Smith or Piers Starter?' Klein obliged, and nearly a million people voted, with 96% choosing the Prime Minister.

Across the Atlantic, the White House was abuzz.

Pump took the calls from admirals privately: a four-star from the 2nd Fleet, a three-star from the 7th, even a marine general. All furious and all warning him that Bill Smith wasn't some eccentric retiree; he was one of theirs. He'd been decorated in half a dozen wars that are admitted, and fourteen more that aren't. One admiral's voice broke as he said: 'Mr President, that man saved my life in Iran fifteen years ago.'

Pump let the silence stretch, then replied resolutely, 'Then we'll make sure he isn't forgotten.'

Only after the calls did he wave in Vice President Manse. He had served in the military and had noticed the Legion of Merit among Bill's ribbons. But Pump cut him off.

'It's been a busy morning. I've had admirals from two fleets on the phone and a marine general to boot. This guy Smith is one of the most decorated sailors of his generation. He even helped us in Iran a few years ago. And Starter has just had him arrested on live TV.'

Manse blinked. 'I didn't even know there was action in Iran.'

‘Exactly,’ Pump said, leaning forward. ‘And we need to keep it that way.’

He tapped the desk. ‘Starter thinks he’s killed the Buccaneers. But he’s just given us the perfect hand. I’ve got a plan, but it might need to ripen overnight.’

Out at sea, the Dwight D Eisenhower strike group slowed as it passed the Straits of Gibraltar, then swung north.

Chapter 37
Homecoming

Micah and Gabriella had a few days with their families before heading back to Naylor for their final year. To begin with, neither of them realised how much attention their time in England had attracted across the Atlantic.

The Chair of the Joint Chiefs of Staff himself had called President David at Naylor and then Micah's parents. The message was clear: when Micah graduated, the military wanted first refusal. His work in communications and public relations had impressed even the most hardened generals.

'You can't join the others on the front line, honey,' his mother told him later, eyes brimming with pride. 'But the PR war is important too.'

Gabriella's phone was also full of unexpected messages. Among them was one forwarded by President David – from the Governor of Michigan – asking whether she would consider becoming her spokesperson after graduation.

Before leaving for Naylor, Gabriella sat with her mother on the porch. The evening air was soft, cicadas buzzing somewhere down the street.

'You know,' Gabriella said thoughtfully, 'if we hadn't gone to England, I don't think I would ever have truly understood how God made me.

Her mother smiled, delighted by her daughter's new confidence, though it would take her time to work through the memory of the firebombing.

Back at Naylor, the two slipped gratefully into the rhythms of their final year. Gabriella threw herself into classes. Her prayer triplet listened wide-eyed as she recounted stories of the summer and especially to the tale of the 'non-date' in Boulogne with Ryan.

Micah's dorm gave him a hero's welcome. As he walked in, he was greeted by banners strung across the hallway: 'Retired Women Love Micah.' Somehow news of his success at the Women's Institute had crossed the Atlantic.

President David, meanwhile, was quietly satisfied. Applications to Naylor had surged, fuelled by curiosity about the students who had succeeded while weathering an international storm.

That evening, after walking the grounds, he slipped into the small campus chapel. He knelt for a moment, then sat back in the front pew, hands folded, thinking of Micah and Gabriella. How was it that two students from such ordinary beginnings could end up shaping headlines across the world? He smiled to himself. God had a habit of doing that: a fisherman, a tax collector, a carpenter's son. People overlooked, until the moment came when the world could no longer ignore them.

Chapter 38
American Moves

When Pump went in, he went in hard. The message on X was unequivocal:

'I am announcing today that the US Navy will begin safety operations in the English Channel. Seventy-five years ago the United Sates joined the UK and France as our heroic ancestors liberated Europe. Now I'm instructing our military to end illegal migration across the Channel. It's time for these people to go home! Thank you for your attention in this matter.'

With one tweet President Pump dropped himself squarely into the Buccaneer story. Sir Piers Starter was stunned. The French President was aghast. The British public, however, were relieved. The vice-grip was back on.

The Vicar walked his dog, Tess, along the beach the next morning. As dawn broke, he was stunned to see eleven US naval vessels, including a 333 metre aircraft carrier, anchored off the Deal coast. They had appeared overnight like spaceships after a hyperjump. Even a mile out they towered over the horizon. Pump wanted the US Navy to act on the French shore, but he wanted them anchored as close to England as possible. It wasn't only the smugglers who were going to feel the heat.

'Crumbs. He really meant it,' the Vicar said to himself. As the wind stiffened, he felt oddly reassured to see the fleet there. But not everyone shared this relief. Pierre launched an eleven metre dinghy that morning thinking the Buccaneers' suspension was a godsend. He never made it out of the shallows. A US Marine vessel rammed his boat at speed and four migrants were killed instantly. Further north the Marines decided the safest way to stop a dinghy leaving a beach was to shoot it from a helicopter. Pump made sure the bodycams were active for all operations.

By evening, news of the Marines' heavy-handed approach spread around the world, aided and abetted by leaked bodycam images. The pictures were harrowing, but Pump moved to stage two of his plan. With Marine One whirring in the background, he took questions.

'Mr President, do you have a comment on the four deaths in the English Channel this morning?'

'Yes,' Pump replied, hands thrust forward. 'These are very stupid people. They should all turn around and go home. Everyone knows this is a stupid and unsafe thing to do. The Channel is now closed – it is over.'

A few moments later he offered softer words and condolences, but no one reported those sentiments. Liberal opinion worldwide exploded in outrage. One victim was Afghan, another Iranian, another Eritrean, another Albanian. Their embassies lodged loud protests in Washington.

Yet that outrage carried his message far and wide, exactly as Pump intended. Neither he nor the Buccaneers, on their own, could reach into the interior of poorer countries where migrants began their journeys. Outraged opinion, however, did just that. Disgust and horror spread the warning. The Buccaneers had been an Anglophone story at best, European at a stretch; now the whole world was listening.

Instantly smuggler phones went silent. It was one thing to risk a crossing against the weather; quite another to risk being shot at on the beach from a Blackhawk. Where Pierre usually had a dozen clients messaging for places, that morning he had none.

The US presence created a new kind of pressure. The French were appalled to see US helicopters firing on their beaches. From being reluctant to make a joint security pact with the UK, they now became desperate. Anything to get the Americans away. Starter, meanwhile, was still locked in legal concerns.

Every Wednesday the Prime Minister must take questions in the House of Commons. This week the chamber was packed and Starter was pressed repeatedly about US action in the Channel. British pride was piqued; he played for time. When pushed about the Buccaneers he fell back on his line: 'The law is the law.'

Randy Hooger, the Deal MP, drew a high slot and chose his moment carefully. In the end he simply asked, 'Does the Prime Minister support the extradition of my constituent, decorated Royal Navy veteran Bill Smith?'

'The law is the law,' Starter repeated, as if addressing slow children.

Hooger's follow-up turned out to be pure theatre: 'Will the Prime Minister ever let the British people fight to secure their country?'

The Commons erupted. Roars from the opposition and even shouts from Starter's own benches. On later news clips he looked awkward and strained, facing an angry, humiliated house. MPs were incredulous that the US Navy could act while the Royal Navy was being kept in port.

It wasn't only MPs losing patience. In Number Ten the First Sea Lord, Admiral Jenkins, waited for the PM to return. Starter tried to be welcoming, but Jenkins refused to sit. He launched into a slow, blistering tirade, beginning with Bill Smith's shabby treatment and his extraordinary service to Crown and country. Jenkins protested the humiliation of the Royal Navy by their American counterparts. Starter sensed where this was going; he wasn't surprised when Jenkins said that if the Navy was not allowed to fight, it was worthless and in good conscience, he would be duty bound to resign.

At that exact moment Starter's private line rang with a call from the US. He asked for the room to be cleared.

'Mr President,' he began, with forced cheer.

Pump was all crocodile smiles. ‘Tough gig you have there Piers. I don’t know how you face them each week.’

‘All part of the democratic process,’ Starter replied.

Pump took off the gloves. ‘Do you think your guys could do a better job in the Channel?’

Starter snapped without thinking. ‘Yes. Frankly, I do.’ He cursed himself the moment the words left his mouth; he’d walked straight into Pump’s trap.

Pump purred. ‘Well, maybe, maybe not. See, our guys are keen to get home. If the Royal Navy steps in, they could be gone by nightfall. No more helicopters, no more shooting. All you have to do is announce the joint security pact with France, get patrols going, and Uncle Sam will be on his merry way.’

Starter hesitated. Pump let the silence sit; he knew when to wait.

‘Of course,’ Pump added, casually offering a carrot, ‘I could come over to that human-rights conference in Paris and throw the full weight of the US behind it.’

‘In Bonn, you mean?’ Starter blinked.

‘It was in Bonn,’ Pump said, ‘but Macaroon agreed to move it to Paris, if yours truly came.’

Starter had invested heavily in a conference aimed at amending the European Convention on Human Rights. Its original purpose had been distorted over the years, now often invoked to block the legitimate deportation of illegal migrants. Public patience was wearing thin across Europe. Any amendment required unanimous support from the original signatories, and since Brexit, the UK’s voice – though still respected – carried less weight. As a human-rights lawyer, Starter knew how to amend the treaty; as a politician, he knew he was pushing uphill. US support could tip the balance. Yet he still had a nagging question: ‘And what do you get out of this, Ronald? It’s not exactly a strategic US priority.’

’

Pump chuckled. 'I'm just in it for the good of humanity and a few good photos in Paris. I still want that Nobel Prize, remember. Drop the charges against Bill Smith, announce a deal with France and you have my word we'll work to get your treaty over the line. Everyone wins.'

Starter's mind whirred. Pump sounded sincere and the Admiral was waiting outside. In the end he ceded to pragmatism.

'Great job, Piers. Make the announcement and we're out of there.'

Jenkins was ushered back in. 'As I was saying,' Starter began, 'I agree with everything you say. Let's get the joint security zone agreed and announced. When could the Navy be ready?'

Jenkins, taken aback by the PM's U-turn, decided to make his own and try and help. He could have replied sarcastically that the Navy had been ready six months ago. But now, tactfully, he reported that patrols could start in the morning.

Starter nodded. 'Then let me call the French.'

President Macaroon picked up at the first ring. He had been trying to get through all day and was visibly relieved. 'I agree to everything. Get those American killers off our beaches! France is humiliated and passions are running high. The Royal Navy will do a fine job. We'll send a few patrols over to Dover in return; I'm sure you understand.'

'Excellent,' Starter said. 'Shall we announce at six?'

'As soon as you like.'

Chapter 39
Tides and Ledgers

September 1st marked a new season in the Channel. The Royal Navy had formally assumed command of the patrols, now hugging the French coast. On paper, the handover promised continuity, but everyone sensed a new professionalism. The improvisation of the Buccaneer era was out; uniforms, hierarchies and procedures were in.

By September, Primark's July royalties had landed: fourteen million pounds in a single month. The figures were staggering. At the bar, Dave scribbled the number on a beer mat and passed it round to murmurs of disbelief.

For the first time since the whole adventure began, the Buccaneers dared to imagine that life might, in some strange way, return to normal.

And yet, across Britain, something indefinable had shifted. Before the summer, the public had tended to expect *them* to act – someone else, somewhere else. But the brave band of volunteers had shown another way: that *we* could make a difference. Once, only other people's money, disguised as taxes, could be put to work. Now, across the country, people were beginning to wonder how their own resources might bring change. What had begun as a private crusade had become a national cause, and in doing so, it had subtly reshaped how the country thought about itself.

Bill, after a couple of weeks of legal limbo, was finally released. The French had huffed, the lawyers had puffed, but in the end Washington's shadow loomed too large. He returned quietly to Deal, though not unchanged. His friends urged him to improve his security and for once he took their advice. A new gate appeared in the garden; small red lights blinked through the night like watchful eyes.

The Vicar, observing it all from the margins, decided to make a change too. The migrants' memorial in church had served its purpose, even with the five recent additions. The candles, faces and prayers had marked a summer of courage and years of loss. But after Remembrance Sunday, he thought, it would be the right time to retire the display. Not to forget, but to fold those memories gently into the larger story of sacrifice.

With the summer behind them and the sea calm once more, attention turned to another kind of tide: the one that flowed through accounts, ledgers, and plans for what would come next.

Alan now had his head down in a different kind of war. Numbers, transfers, bitcoin wallets; the strange alchemy of turning cash into something that could move freely across borders. Leslie teased him about becoming a tech wizard, but she studied just as hard. If they were going to Afghanistan, they needed to be fluent in money.

Over several evenings at the bar, the Buccaneers had debated what to do with the Primark royalties. In the end, their plan was surprisingly simple. First, to repay Colin and Alan for the support they had given. Second, to offer the paid members of the crew a month's bonus in recognition of their success. And third, to place the remaining funds in a new trust, designed to invest in small businesses across the six countries that had sent the most migrants. Alan's forthcoming trip to Afghanistan would serve as a trial run.

At the bar one night, Bill had joked about joining them. 'The problem is,' he said drily, 'too many people might want to take me out.' They laughed, but they all knew it wasn't entirely a joke. It was, in a way, a relief that they now understood more of his naval career – at least the parts he could talk about.

All of this assumed that Alan and Leslie would actually be able to travel. Visas remained the sticking point. Applications had been filed, papers checked and interviews promised. Yet the weeks slipped by with no approval and them stuck in Deal. Leslie had even had her photograph taken in a headscarf, to Alan's private amusement. Still, as autumn drew in, they lived in hope.

Chapter 40
A Paris Thanksgiving

The midterms went better than expected for President Pump. America remained balanced on a knife-edge, yet he could claim some momentum.

The Paris trip had been scheduled for Thanksgiving, much to the irritation of the family diary and the entire bubble that travelled with him. Nobody was particularly keen. But when Pump casually mentioned at dinner that the French Buccaneer, Philippe, would be attending the gala reception at the Louvre, everything changed. His granddaughter signed up first, followed by her cousins, then their parents. Finally, Melinda, with a sidelong glance, remarked that Thanksgiving in Paris might be rather romantic. By morning, staff rosters were mysteriously full, Carolyn Nevis, the press secretary, among the new additions. What had begun as a poorly timed duty was now shaping up to be a Parisian treat.

Pump had promised Sir Piers he would back the human-rights conference, and he kept his word. In the weeks leading up to the visit, he worked the phones – flattering, cajoling, and offering favours where they would do the most good. What had once seemed a doubtful revision to the Convention now looked all but inevitable.

Air Force One touched down at Orly, the airport reserved for state visits. The motorcade swept into the city, sirens wailing, flags fluttering in the wind.

The summit exceeded expectations. Three clauses of the Convention were reframed – 'keeping the intention of the law, while removing the abuse of the law,' as Sir Piers put it, clumsily but accurately. With the formalities complete, everyone looked forward to the evening reception.

Guests descended the spiral staircase beneath I. M. Pei's glass pyramid, flashes popping as photographers jostled for position. Champagne flowed; marble shone. Melinda looked radiant and Pump's granddaughters dazzled in their gowns. The President endured photographs with Gérard Depardieu and a carousel of French grandees.

'Grandpa,' whispered Tai, sidling up, 'I got stuck with our ambassador to Denmark. He made a fortune in plastics – boring!'

'It may be dull,' Pump murmured, 'but he's a major donor, so be charming.'

He turned to his hosts. 'Where's this Philippe fellow? And who's he bringing, by the way? There's rather a lot of interest in this guy.'

'He confirmed he'd come weeks ago,' came the reply, 'but no one seems to know his guest.'

Pump frowned. He had timed his entrance to steal the spotlight, but to arrive this late was stretching things. One granddaughter had even tried to smuggle in her copy of *Vanity Fair* for Philippe to sign; Pump had vetoed it, but he still needed the man himself to appear.

Then the mood in the hall shifted. Heads turned. At the top of the staircase stood Philippe with Bill beside him. Bill wore a dark naval uniform, ribbons neatly in line; Philippe, by contrast, looked every inch the film star: hair swept back, ease in every movement. The flashbulbs went wild.

Halfway down Bill paused to tie a shoe, discreetly yielding the stage to his friend. Philippe took the remaining steps and the runway alone: one hundred feet of effortless theatre. Later, Tai would sigh, 'That was the best hundred-foot walk of my life.'

Bill crossed to Pump and they shook hands warmly. 'Thank you for getting me out,' Bill said. 'I'm grateful.' Pump smiled. 'And we are grateful for your service. And your discretion.' They both laughed and fell into easy conversation about the summer's adventures.

Meanwhile Philippe held the room. Madame Macaroon teased him that his plus-one was a disappointment. 'You'll be mobbed the moment we let you go,' she said – and she was right. He leaned graciously into every selfie with unforced charm; most of the women beside him looked slightly dizzy, certainly delighted.

The cameras caught Melinda laughing with Philippe, her expression genuinely joyful. Pump didn't seem to mind. 'It's a tough job being First Lady,' he told his aides later.

Sir Piers then arrived, almost unobserved, but on a high after the Treaty revision. Only at the reception did he discover the price of Paris: the privilege of hosting had been secured on condition of Philippe's attendance and the five-year Anglo-French security accord. He felt it should have been for the common good, but on the other hand, a win was a win. He let it pass. Looking around at the champagne, the venue and the palpable relief, he left later for the embassy quietly satisfied.

Back at Naylor, the students went home for Thanksgiving break. Micah and Gabriella, in their separate homes, watched the Louvre reception on CNN, anchors replaying Philippe's descent again and again, the flashbulbs illuminating him like a star on the silver screen.

'An Officer and a Gentleman,' Micah said under his breath, shaking his head. He couldn't decide if he liked or loathed him.

Gabriella enjoyed the spectacle, watching with her sisters. She enjoyed explaining the different appeal of Philippe and Bill: one smouldering, one steady. 'They are such a good team, that is why it works.'

‘Can we just watch?’ pleaded her sisters. ‘Life’s not all about PR, you know.’

Jake and Matt, also home, decided to mock up a meme for their brother. They took Philippe’s photo on the staircase and added a placard: ‘Senior Women for Micah – Paris Chapter.’ For once, Micah laughed louder than anyone.

Ryan Davis, who had written previously about the Buccaneers, published his article about Gabriella that weekend. The picture from their trip graced the cover of *The Sunday Times* magazine. He’d called the article: ‘The Word Warrior’ and more than anyone else he captured her spirit. Gabriella’s mother read the article with pride and interest.

‘Honey, I like this guy, Ryan. I’ve been married thirty years, and your father doesn’t know me this well. If Ryan can read you like this after only three months, he’s a keeper.’

Chapter 41
The Pharmacy at Lashkargah

The circular descent into Kabul was like stepping into another century. Dust hung in the air; mountains ringed the city; the airport hummed with Taliban guards and anxious families waiting at the barriers. Alan and Leslie blinked into the hard brightness.

For three nights they stayed in a nearby hotel to acclimatise. The air smelled of smoke and cardamom, the generator thudding through the evenings. Every meal felt both a reassurance and a risk, yet Leslie was oddly calm. Alan, meanwhile, was restless; already filling a notebook with figures on pharmacy stock and supply chains.

On the fourth morning they took a taxi south, down the long road to Lashkargah. The driver was silent, eyes flicking to the mirrors as he steered round convoys and checkpoints. Flat desert gave way, now and then, to sudden bursts of green where irrigation channels ran.

Abdul was waiting. Their first greeting was awkward: hands half-extended, uncertain whether to shake or embrace. But formality soon melted into warmth. He ushered them inside, tea steaming, bread warm, cushions lined along the wall.

Abdul, unmarried, seemed to possess half a football team of nephews and nieces. They swarmed around the visitors, shrieking with delight. The little faces brought unexpected joy, especially to Leslie, who found herself laughing at all their games.

Alan was in his element. He listened more than he spoke, weighing Abdul's plans: inventory systems, refrigeration and reliable suppliers. The scheme, as the Buccaneers had designed it, was ingenious. The first funds came as a grant, the risk borne by the Trust; but if the business prospered, repayments flowed into a revolving pool to finance the next overseas investments.

'Not aid,' Alan reminded Abdul calmly as the deal was sealed. 'And not charity either. Just capital, to unlock what you already know how to do.'

Abdul smiled. He had ideas. Plenty of them.

For this first visit, Alan relied on old-fashioned methods. A hidden compartment in his bag slid open to reveal twenty thousand dollars in crisp notes. Abdul's eyes widened. Later, transfers would go digital with Bitcoin and secure wallets. But for the moment, cash remained king.

Two days later, Alan and Leslie stood in the family pharmacy. A young woman entered carrying a boy of about six, his forehead damp with fever. She hesitated until Abdul greeted her, then he set to work measuring out antibiotics. Alan watched as he explained the medicine slowly and clearly. The woman's shoulders eased; the boy looked faintly hopeful as she lifted him onto her hip.

Abdul turned back, pride flickering in his expression. 'This,' he said quietly, 'is why we are pharmacists. Not only for business, but for them.'

Alan nodded. It had been a good visit. He and Leslie were sorry, in some ways, to leave. As it turned out, they would return many times over the next few years.

Bill could not travel to many countries as his former 'excursions' made that unwise. But Dave, Colin and Alan fanned out across the world, modestly trying to make a difference. Alan and Colin both repaid their own loans into the Trust, when they saw the good that it did.

In the years that followed, the Trust invested more than twenty-three million pounds into a thousand small businesses across six countries: Afghanistan, Iraq, Syria, Sudan, Somalia and Iran.

The range of grants was astonishing: textile workshops, bicycle repair shops, brick kilns, call centres, fisheries, bakeries. They favoured enterprises that employed many hands. By cautious estimates, more than a hundred thousand jobs were created from the investments born of the Primark royalties, making home a more attractive place to stay.

What struck all of them on their travels was the sheer capability of the people they met. Far from being helpless or hopeless, they were inventive, resourceful and disciplined. What they lacked was not talent but access to capital. Once that barrier was lifted, they leapt forward. It was not aid, nor was it patronage. It was investment with dignity.

And in Lashkargah, Abdul's pharmacy became a model – shelves full, medicines cool, children treated. His nephews and nieces darted in and out, proof that tomorrow could, after all, be healthier than today.

Chapter 42
A Win-Win

The following Spring at Naylor, Micah and Gabriella were deep into their final year, exams looming ever closer. One morning in chapel, a group of students just back from their Lighthouse trip to Peru shared their dream: to raise $10,000 to build a small school for primary-aged children, who were currently living on the street. They had already scraped together $3,000 – a heroic effort for undergraduates – but they were asking for prayer for the remaining $7,000.

Gabriella felt her heartstrings tug. 'I'd love to help,' she thought, 'but I haven't even got ten spare dollars, let alone ten thousand.'

Then she heard someone behind her.

'Who says?'

She turned round, but everyone in the row behind was chatting among themselves. She frowned, how strange.

That afternoon, her phone buzzed with a UK number.

'Hello, is this Gabriella?'

'Yes, speaking. Who's this, please?'

'Oh, this is Noah Bertrand, from Goalhanger Media in London. We wondered if you might be able to help us?'

Gabriella listened attentively. Apparently, Gary Lineker, football legend, had been following the Buccaneers ever since the World Cup, fascinated by the overseas trust they'd established. The Blair-like idea of being 'tough on the boats, tough on the causes of the boats' had struck a chord. One of his Goalhanger podcasts, *The Rest is Politics: Leading*, wanted to interview Alan.

But there was a problem. Alan was difficult to reach: he never returned calls, his mobile number was a mystery and he had a gift for vanishing.

'But if you could persuade him,' Noah said hopefully, 'We'd pay £5,000 for the interview.'

Gabriella did the mental maths. £5,000 was almost exactly $7,000 – the sum the Peru project needed. 'Well,' she said slowly, 'let me see what I can do.'

In Deal, at six that evening, Alan was exactly where Gabriella imagined he would be: at the Buccaneers' Bar.

'And then at work today,' Alan was saying, pint in hand, 'I get a message from Gary ruddy Lineker! The great tweeter from on high wants me to go on one of his podcasts.' He clearly found this hilarious, warming to his theme. 'Imagine it – me, sitting down with Blair's Bully and the Smug-a-tron. No, that's not happening, not in a thousand years.'

His friends roared with laughter. For all their respect for Lineker's playing career, his tweeting divided opinion and in the Buccaneers' crowd, the reactionaries had the floor.

Alan's phone pinged. He smiled. 'A voice message from my favourite American. You know, if I had a daughter, I'd want her to be like Gabriella. Competent, steely, pretty…' he paused. 'Just like me!'

When the laughter subsided, Dave leaned forward. 'Well, play it then.'

Alan tapped the screen. Gabriella's voice filled the bar. 'Hello Alan, hello guys. I'm guessing I know where you are! Anyway, Goalhanger have just rung me. They want to interview you, Alan, about the summer and the new Trust. They're offering £5,000. And, funnily enough, this morning someone in chapel asked for exactly that amount to fund a school for street children in Peru. Maybe this could be a win-win? Message me!'

Alan groaned. 'Not likely.' He typed a polite but firm, 'No.'

But Gabriella was sharper than he gave her credit for. Within minutes, another message appeared:

'Maybe I could just pass your number on to Goalhanger, so you can deal with them directly?'

Alan went pale. He was of an age when mobile numbers were guarded with care. He read the message aloud in the bar to his friends.

'Clever girl,' said Bill, always quick to spot a tactical advantage.

'Well, well, well,' Dave crowed. 'Look who's going to be on a podcast.'

Alan tried to scowl but couldn't hide his smile. 'Fine,' he texted. 'Say yes, but don't give them this number. Tell them to use the work line. And I'm only up for it if they pay every penny to your school in Peru.'

Gabriella's reply came seconds later: a halo emoji.

Alan feigned disappointment. 'See, lads, once again I am being manipulated by the fairer sex. And that Gabriella – she really is very good at it.'

Chapter 43
Answered Prayers

Remembrance Sunday came and went. The Buccaneers and their wives stood respectfully at the parade in Deal. The names carved into the memorial were read aloud, each syllable carrying the weight of sacrifice.

But this year, for the first time, alongside the fallen of two world wars came another list: the 152 men, women and children who had perished trying to cross the Channel. The Vicar began with Maryam Ali and then the names of twenty-six others; the rest were simply listed as 'Name Unknown'. When the name Duwana Abdo was spoken, Bill stared into the distance, jaw set, eyes unreadable.

On Monday morning, the Vicar carefully packed away the migrant's memorial with the help of the churchwardens. It felt like the end of an era, but not in a bad way. A season had closed and something new was beginning.

The next day, he set out with Tess for their usual walk along the shore. It was a cold, dry November day, the sky just beginning to brighten, the sea restless in the half-light. Tess started barking, bringing back memories of that morning three years ago when she had found a body in the surf. The Vicar's heart lurched, 'What now?'

But this time, it was not a dead body, but a man, shivering, ragged and homeless sitting beneath a sheet of plastic.

'Easy, Tess,' the Vicar murmured. He crouched down and pressed a Greggs gift card into the man's hand. He always carried them for occasions like this. 'There's a Greggs in town; it opens at seven. That should get you a good breakfast.' The man offered his thanks and they continued, Tess trotting ahead.

As they walked, the last three years began to come into focus. He remembered his simple, heartfelt prayer: 'Lord, please stop this madness.' And then thought of all that followed: Alan and Leslie, Colin and Miranda, Dave and Laura, Bill with his strength and scars. Gabriella and Micah; their courage and their passion. The highs and lows of the summer. The terrifying night attack and Sir Francis Drake's prayer. Even the US President getting involved. And finally, the Royal Navy stepping up to patrol.

Looking back, he could see God's hand in it all; arranging, guiding and protecting.

He sat down on the cold shingle, overwhelmed with wonder. A verse from the Psalms rose unbidden: 'This is the Lord's doing and it is marvellous in our sight.'

Afterword

Between 2018 and 2025, more than 160,000 people have crossed the English Channel in small boats. At least 152 are known to have died – though both figures are estimates, and the true toll is almost certainly higher.

On the night of 24 November 2021, a small boat left the French coast at around 10 pm, carrying just over thirty people. There were no smugglers on board. Two Egyptian migrants were handed a GPS, shown how to operate the outboard motor, and pointed towards England. Sometime in the middle of the Channel, the boat began taking on water. In the early hours it capsized.

Distress calls were made to both the English and French coastguards. A rescue vessel was dispatched and located three other boats in the area, but not 'Charlie' – the one that had overturned. The following afternoon, a French family out fishing discovered one of two survivors, drifting in the open water, which was just 13°C.

Twenty-eight people lost their lives that night – the worst disaster in the English Channel since *The Herald of Free Enterprise* in 1987.

British media rarely reports the names of migrants who have died. They are recorded as statistics, not stories. Their names remain known only to their families – and to God.

So, who was on that little boat in November 2021?

From Iraqi Kurdistan came a family of four. They had already made three attempts to cross. Hadiya, 22, dreamed of becoming a doctor; her English was perfect. She died with her mother, Kazhal Ahmed Khidhir Al-Jammoor, 46; her brother, Mubin, 16; and little Hasti, aged 7.

Three best friends from Rania – Rezhwan Yasin Hassan, 19, a carpenter; Zanyar Mustafa Mina, 20; and Mohammed Qadir Aulla, 21 – they messaged home from a shared phone on the bus to the beach. From the same town came Afrasia Ahmed Mohammed, 27, a top student.

Eight other friends and acquaintances were on that same bus. Among them:

• Pshtiwan Rasul Farka, 18, who left school at 9 to help pay for his sister's heart treatment; his body was never found.

• Twana Mamand Mohammed, 18, a footballer and black belt in Taekwondo; again, never recovered.

• Mohammed Hussein Mohammedie, 19, whose parents received his body back at Erbil Airport on what would have been his 20th birthday.

• "Hybar" Bryar Hamad Abdulrahman, 23, who left school at 14 because his family could no longer afford it.

• Serkawt Pirot Mohammed, 28, nicknamed "Harem" by his grandmother.

• Shakar Ali Pirot, 30, a geology graduate unable to find work in that field in Iraq.

• Hassan Mohammed Ali, 37, from Qaladiza.

• Sirwan Alipour, 23, from Sardasht, Iran.

Two women were travelling together: 'Baran' Maryam Noori Mohammedameen, 24, from Iraq, was trying to reach her fiancé Karzan, a barber in Bournemouth. With her was Mhabad Ahmad Ali, 32, from Erbil – a mother of two small children whose husband was already in the UK.

Also among the dead were Bilind Shukir Baker, 20; Muslim Ismael Hamad, 19; and Mohammed Qadar Awla, 18. Most of their families provided DNA to French authorities, allowing their bodies to be flown together to Erbil Airport in late December.

Others were from Africa:

• Halima Mohamed Shikh, 33, a mother of three from Somalia.

• Fikiru Shiferaw, 46, from Addis Ababa, Ethiopia – a father of two whose widow Emebet said, 'His beliefs were based on God's word and sharing…His hobbies were cooking and reading. He was the best cook I know.'

• Meron Hailu Gebrehiwot, from Adigrat, Ethiopia, who studied computer science at Addis Ababa University and fled the war in Tigray in 2020 after Adigrat was bombed.

• Niyat Ferede Yeshiwendi, 22, also from Tigray, was deeply spiritual – a woman of prayer, devoted to helping others. She had begun studying pharmacy at Sheba University. Because of the war, her body could not be returned home; she rests in Lille, France.

There were two survivors: Mohammed Shekha Ahmad and Issa Mohammed Omar. One saw a Vietnamese man and a small girl on board; the other recalled an Egyptian father and son operating the boat and a young boy struggling in the water. None of those bodies were recovered, and their names remain unknown, such is the chaotic nature of these crossings. For further details, search online for 'The Cranston Enquiry'.

Behind every statistic is a name; behind every name, a story; and behind every story, a family who grieves.

The tragedy of 24 November 2021 is not fiction – it is one of the wounds that inspired *Channel Tides*.

If there is any lesson to draw, perhaps it is this: compassion and courage are not opposites. Both are forms of love in action – and both are needed if we are ever to calm the waters of the Channel.